YOUR MANY LURID FATES

Your Many Lurid Fates

Stories

BRIAN CONNEL

Thin Rain Press

For Haley

CONTENTS

Burn Victim

Why am I here? I guess that's a good place to start. You already know why I'm here, but it's important that I know why I'm here, right?

I was in a car accident. I'm sure you've read all about it in my file. I was driving home from work on 22nd Street. It was rush hour. The traffic was thick but moving. You know 22nd Street. You're from Tucson, right? It's wide and straight and flat. It's easy to build up a good head of steam.

I was trying to turn left onto Kolb. I was first in line, and I was already out in the intersection waiting for traffic to slow at the yellow light. There was an 18-wheeler looking to turn left opposite me, blocking my view of oncoming traffic. The cars in the lanes next to me had already stopped for the light, so I went for it. But a pickup truck, a shiny new black one, came roaring through the intersection, red lights be damned.

I saw it only at the last second and floored it thinking I could get out of its way in time. It hit the trunk of my car, between the gas tank hatch and the back bumper. I spun out, did a 360 in the intersection. All the windows blew out. So did the back tires. The airbags popped. But I was ok. I got out of the car on my own.

A couple of cops showed up in minutes. One of them was a garrulous fat guy with big Oakley sunglasses. He was very excited about the whole thing.

"You're goddamn lucky!" he said. My rear bumper had gotten knocked a full 200 feet down the road. He said that judging by the skid marks and the fact that it took the pickup 100 feet to come to a stop, it was probably going 55 miles an hour when it hit me. The cop whistled and shook his head and said: "Son, if he'd hit you just a few inches to the right, over your rear axle, you would have rolled a few times and ended up where your bumper is. We would have had to jaws-of-life you out and everything. And if he'd full-on T-boned you, like hit you dead on—" he exhaled like he was blowing out a candle — "your car would've exploded. Maybe not in a big fire ball, but like that bird Randy Johnson creamed over home plate. Just feathers."

He kept going on about Randy Johnson and an exploded-bird-level wreck on Valencia the other day, but I stopped hearing everything. By now there was a backup at least a mile long in every direction. The engines, the horns, the exhaust, the heat rising off the pavement… It all made me swoon.

And then suddenly I was back in the car. My hair was sticky with blood and there was crushed glass in my lap and my vision was fluid and wavy like everything was on tape delay. I could feel this heat building by my feet, climbing up my legs like an army of ants. I gripped the steering wheel, trying to bend it, I guess, throwing my torso back and forth and groaning in vain. Then the heat turned into something else. Something like panic. Now

I was smacking the steering wheel, flailing, screaming. Words at first, then just sounds. Sounds I didn't recognize or even think were my own.

And then I smelled it.

My legs were… melting, the oils and fats dripping in globs from my bones like the wax of some heinous scented candle. The fire slithered up from under the steering wheel like flames on a gas stove, wispy and shimmery like a mirage. I started craning my neck back, lifting my chin, shaking my head like a toddler avoiding a spoonful of food, my arms overhead pressed tensely against the crumpled, jagged roof.

And just like that I was back in the intersection. The fat cop was still there, snapping his fingers in my face and patting me on the cheek. He waved down the paramedics. One of them flashed a light in my eyes and asked me what day it was and did the how-many-fingers thing. She insisted on giving me a neck brace and taking me to the hospital.

The thing is — and this is the key thing that everyone keeps ignoring — I didn't *imagine* the burning car. I was actually — literally — in the burning car. I remember it just as well as I re-member stepping out of the car unharmed. I can still… smell it.

I knew that something wasn't right. I had this weird double vision in the ambulance. There were two paramedics in the back with me. Not two different paramedics, mind you. The same paramedic twice. One of them was sitting in the jump seat, play-ing on her phone. The other one was standing over me, squeez-ing a respirator in one hand, holding onto an IV stand with the other. I could feel the air flow over my nose and mouth, feel the outline of the respirator mask. But when I reached up to feel my face... there was nothing there.

When they wheeled me into the ER — the identical twin paramedics — one of them signed a clip board and walked away while the other was joined by a crowd of people in scrubs, frantically saying things like "burn victim," "50 cc's" of this or that, "blood pressure dropping," "stat." But slowly the phantom doctors started to... dissolve. Into the air. Their voices faded as if receding down a tunnel. The last thing I heard was a nurse shouting that my belt had fused to my skin.

Just then a nurse came and told me that he would be taking me in for a CT scan any minute. He asked if there was anyone they could call for me. But I couldn't answer him. My mouth hung open, and I gulped like a fish out of water because his voice was the same voice that had just announced the fusion of my belt to my body.

Have you figured it out yet?

Here's my theory: When you die, you simply wake up in your own body, just in an adjacent timeline. Typically, this assimilation is seamless, and any awareness of your other life is relegated to dreams, phobias, and the most uncanny of déjà vu. In my case, though... something went wrong. Instead of just assimilating, my terminated consciousness supplanted the other one — this one — the one that was unharmed on 22nd Street.

Do you see now? *I* am the burn victim, resurrected in this unburned body.

I tried to make sense of it while I was lying inside the CT scan machine, wondering why I got placed in this timeline. Surely there is more than just the uninjured vs. burn victim timelines.

What about the timeline where the 18-wheeler wasn't there and I could see the pickup coming? Or what about the timeline where I was going just a little faster and the pickup missed me altogether? I wondered if there was a karmic aspect to it; if I'd been a better person, would I have come to in a better timeline? One in which I got home with no worries, my girlfriend waiting for me on the terrace with a cold beer. Or if I'd been a worse person, would I have been sent to a timeline in which I'd survived the crash but was all maimed and disabled, writhing in pain in the burn unit? Theoretically, given the number of variables involved in that accident, and the number of variables impacting my commute that day, there are an infinite number of different timelines I could have assimilated into. And to be clear, when I say infinite, I don't mean that there's a timeline where dragons or leprechauns appear or something stupid like that. There are parameters. Think of it like a pool table. It is a finite space, a pretty small one, but there are an infinite number of outcomes for how the balls will move over the course of a game.

When they finally got ahold of my girlfriend, she raced over to the hospital and arrived just in time for the scan results. The doctor gave me the all clear and told me I was incredibly lucky. I put on my clothes. My hands were shaking as I cinched up that fucking belt. Julie and I were walking out past the front desk into the waiting room when it occurred to me that Julie was about to drive us. To our apartment. In her car.

I got all panicky. I started panting and crying. I grabbed onto the front desk thinking that someone was going to drag me to the car, blubbering "I'm not going," "you can't make me." Julie started crying, security showed up... it was a whole scene. A doctor came out and wrote me a prescription for some Xanax which I filled at the hospital pharmacy. I ate the whole bar right there in front of the pharmacist just as he was telling me to only take half.

Anyway, I guess Julie got me home alright. At least this version of me. I don't remember much beyond her buckling my seatbelt and the street lights streaking past the window.

Have you ever taken Xanax? I'm sure you dabble here and there, why wouldn't you? It knocks you out hard and tapers off slowly. Waking is like ascending from the ocean floor, floating up languidly, blindly through inky depths. It was in this buoyant limbo that I heard a beeping sound. Not an alarm. Just a gentle, rhythmic beeping. Like a heart rate monitor. Like in a hospital. Like I was still in the hospital.

The panic started to trickle back like water through a cracked dike until suddenly the whole thing burst and I felt myself paralyzed, restrained, my legs on fire, my eyes sealed shut. The beeping got louder, faster, then footsteps, then a click.

I shot up in bed, my own bed, gasping for air. I ripped off the covers and indeed, my legs were still there, skinny and pasty as ever.

I'd slept well into the afternoon. The stillness was jarring. It took me a moment to calm down. I thought it best for me to just put the whole thing out of my head, dismiss the burn victim thing as a trauma response. The burning car, though. The belt. The smell.

I dawdled around the apartment for a bit until I realized I was starving — I hadn't eaten since lunch the day before. There were some grapes in the fridge, so I stood there with the door open pounding a fistful of them.

I'm not sure exactly what it was, maybe a truck backfiring, a door slamming, but some sudden jolt of fright sent a grape down the wrong pipe. It took a second to grasp what was happening, but once my lizard brain got the message it was off to the races. I could feel the grape stuck in my throat and thought maybe I could force it down with some water or something. So I filled up a glass at the sink and chugged the whole thing.

The water went down no problem. There was nothing stuck in my throat. I could breathe just fine. I stood hunched over the sink, clutching the counter and taking big panic breaths, swallowing compulsively just to make sure.

When I turned the sink off, though, I could hear some commotion behind me. I turned around and — get this — the kitchen was crowded with versions of me. Lying on the floor in front of the fridge was *me*. Honest to God, I was looking at myself blue-faced, writhing on the ground with my hands clasped around my throat, my feet flexed and kicking like trying to shed a blanket. But standing in front of the fridge was also me, still eating grapes. And a few feet away I was punching myself in the stomach. Slouched over the kitchen table stood another me, panting and moaning, staring at a coughed up grape.

I clenched my eyes shut, but I could still see the whole scene projected on my eyelids. When I finally opened them, though, it was over. They were all gone.

I made for the door, but in my hurry I stumbled on the area rug that Julie had gotten for our living room. As I recovered my footing, I heard this sound like an egg thrown at a wall and

I had this blinding pain between my eyes. I turned around and lo and behold my living room was littered with a fresh bouquet of corpses centered around the coffee table, the corner of which was so firmly lodged in my skull that gravity couldn't pull my body to the floor. My eyes were still open. All wide and surprised. My lower jaw was slack, and a thin trail of blood dripped off the end of my nose. But on either side of that sorry version of me were other me's that evidently hit the table at slightly different angles and slid or rolled to various final resting places on Julie's new rug.

Some part of me kept backing away until I was standing on the terrace. My apartment is on the second floor and there are these rough concrete stairs to get down to the courtyard. I'm sure you know where this is going.

I had just taken my first step down the stairs when I saw another version of myself *peel* away from me, like step out of me, and — you guessed it — go head first down the stairs. From that version of me fanned out a dozen different tumbling me's, each one on a unique trajectory towards that show-stopping smack to end all smacks. As I watched from the top of the stairs, I could somehow see, simultaneously, as if through my own eyes, the dizzying montage of concrete-sky-concrete-sky, and I could feel, if only ephemerally, every jagged stair, every broken bone, every head-splitting thwack. It was like some kind of hellacious Tour De France pile up: a dozen different versions of myself, all on top of each other at the bottom of the stairs, some groaning, some convulsing, some bleeding out, some ogling the bones sticking out of their skin.

I fell backwards onto my ass and crawled on my hands and knees through my apartment. Back in bed I cowered under the covers hoping that in the darkness I would be safe. By staying absolutely still, by not making any choices at all, I could stop new timelines from being created, and therefore stop the proliferation of ill-fated me's.

But in the darkness it returned… that gentle rhythmic beeping, then more beeps at varied rates, then a symphony of heart monitors, becoming more crowded, louder and louder, until it was nothing but a ghastly shrieking in my ears. I felt myself multiplying exponentially across space-time, propelled through the multiverse at explosive speed, inexorably careening towards a splatter pattern on the concrete wall of destiny.

I could feel it all at once, all the pain and all the horror of an infinite existence.

How many versions of me are out there, maimed, disfigured, disabled, sick, cancerous, bereaved? My car accident alone surely created an unfathomable number of burn victims, each one of them right now, as we speak, howling in pain and fury and primal confusion only a few timelines south of here.

You might ask: But what about all the good timelines?

And to that I say: Don't be fucking obtuse. If you think that somehow the sound of laughter can drown out the cries of your many lurid fates, then I recommend you take a stroll over to the burn unit.

Julie came home and found me nearly catatonic. She insisted I had some kind of head injury and begged me to go with her to the hospital. Of course I resisted, but when she started to cry, the world fractaled like a funhouse mirror, and the din of a million sobbing Julies was enough to make me acquiesce.

Sitting rigid and shivering in the front seat of her car, it all started to make sense to me. With every lane change, every left turn, I saw a kaleidoscope of catastrophes, and within that, the truth: what we call anxiety is merely heat radiating off the burning wreckage of our adjacent timelines. So intense is the suffering that its flames can seep through the veils that partition the multiverse. For some people the veils are thicker, for some they are thinner, but for me they have disappeared altogether, damning me to be broiled alive for all eternity in an inexhaustible cosmic inferno, trapped in the ever-combusting engine of some hideous fourth dimensional machine.

And that's why I'm here.

Power Struggle

The oatmeal Mr. Andrews brought for breakfast makes a sucking sound when he digs his spoon in. He takes a bite and realizes that he can't do it. He snaps the Tupperware lid back on and folds his arms and looks darkly at his window, seeing his reflection rather than the evergreen trees that extend ad infinitum. What fresh hell will Mason Graham bring him today?

It is only the fifth week of school, but Mr. Andrews' patience is wearing thin. A student in his fourth period class has succeeded in pushing him to limits he didn't know he had. In theory, all behavior is communication, but this… For the first time, Mr. Andrews can't see through the behavior and worries, consequently, that there is in fact nothing behind it. Nothing subconscious, traumatic, diagnosable oozing to the surface. Indeed — Mason Graham seems to be doing this for sport. Recreation. Shits and giggles.

He has not given up yet, though. Not quite yet. On his desk, leaning up against a potted succulent, is a small card, still sharp at the corners, featuring only six words: "They are all Jesus in disguise." His inner monologue chants this mantra frantically, like a teary-eyed, ruby-slippered "no place like home," as if to beat back his doubts through sheer force of will. He flips the card over. A portrait of Saint Ignatius of Loyola looks back at him with dour serenity.

Mason is only a child, he tells himself. It must be coming from a place of deep hurt, profound hurt. A healthy child with a life full of love and agency and dignity could never behave this way. It's not personal. It's not personal, he tells himself, the voice in his head belligerent, pounding on the desk it's shouting over to emphasize each word. But it's *so personal.* That's the thing — Mason has entered his mind in a serpentine and violating way. He's taken up residence in Mr. Andrews' psyche like a cockroach infestation; somehow ever-present, invisible, writhing in the walls, forever threatening to creep across his line of sight.

Ultimately, though, wasn't this why he'd come out here? Why he'd left a cushy job at a prestigious Catholic school that catered to the wealthy and high-flying? He wanted to live a life of service, be a big part of a small community, be a force for good. Mason needs him. Mason's classmates need him. They need him, Mr. Andrews, to not give up on them, to care for them unconditionally, to make their success his success.

Has he been tempted to quit? Certainly. Especially since the teeth-grinding, and the neck pain, and the stomach aches, and the nausea upon pulling into the faculty parking lot. Out of the question, though. He's made a commitment. Perhaps he is only being tested, truly challenged, for the first time. What would St. Ignatius say, after all?

He's tried to deal with it on his own, keep it in-house. He's avoided bringing the administration into it, eager to prove his competence, or at least not invite doubt about it. There is no one on faculty who he yet feels he can confide in. The need for support, however, is urgent.

"You're still here?" she asked incredulously. "I thought these kids would have scared you off by now."

The school counselor is an old battle-ax of a woman, one year from retirement, or so he's heard. She has close-cropped gray hair, and her wardrobe seems to be comprised exclusively of gray souvenir t-shirts from national parks and seaside boardwalks. Mr. Andrews is not amused by her quip, anticipated though it was. During the faculty in-service he'd fielded more than a few observations about his age, his perceived Portland prissiness, and even his size. More than one teacher joked about confusing him for a student.

"I'm having difficulty with a student."

"Who?"

"Mason Graham."

"Go figure."

"He's on your radar?"

"He's one to watch."

"What makes you say that?"

"You're here, aren't you?"

Mr. Andrews, making it clear that he is not in the mood, waits intently for her to say something of substance.

"He has a history of being... confrontational," she says, finally, leaning back in her swivel chair. "Nothing serious, though. He's a bright kid."

"I don't doubt that," he says, about him being bright. "He's been very disruptive and unkind in my class. Profoundly disrespectful. Downright cruel to his peers. I was wondering if there was maybe something going on at home that you know about?"

"I really doubt it."

"Why's that?"

"Mason Graham? He's loaded. His family owns the sawmill. And all the timber between here and Eugene. Old money. I mean, you never know. But he rules the roost around here. I'm sure he's doing fine."

"Any advice?" he asks.

"Yeah," she says, "don't drag me into it."

He seeks out Mason's freshman teachers for perspective and advice, popping into their classrooms after school.

"Oh, Mason's a big teddy bear," says Ms. Caldwell. "The other kids bully him because he's so sensitive. You have to let him take breaks. He gets easily overwhelmed. I'd just let him take a break or do a different assignment if he needed it."

"Take a break?"

"Oh, yes. Let him go outside or walk around or play on his phone."

"Mason's really bright," says Ms. Tolan, "but he's got some self-esteem issues. He'll say things like 'I guess I'm just stupid' or 'I'll never be good at anything' so I would always lay on the affirmation. Everyday, just remind him how smart and funny and charming he is and he'll be a star student."

"He's a piece of work," says Mr. Schmitt. "Don't repeat that." He looks around to ensure no one else is within earshot. "I had him in PE, so I just tried to keep him away from the, let's say, *less athletic* kids. We couldn't play dodgeball in his class period. I remember that."

"He's very… externally motivated," says Ms. Higgins. "I figured that out early in the year. I'd make deals with him: if he behaved for the entire week, I'd give him a Starbucks gift card on Friday, or let him pick his seat, or give him some bonus points or something. If he put the laser pointer away I'd give him some candy. Things like that."

"Good luck," says Mr. Kruger. "You're on your own with that one." He shuffles some papers. "I'm actually pretty busy, so…"

He finally seeks counsel from Mr. Sorenson, the special ed teacher and aging Dead Head.

"I've never actually met the kid," he says, "but I know his dad. I used to do this beer league Saturday morning softball thing and he would show up sometimes. Major asshole. Category 5 asshole. Sore loser like you wouldn't believe. Temper tantrums, throwing his glove, you name it. And this was a freaking beer league, man. The worst thing was that everyone just had to roll over because half the people in this town work for him. You know he owns the sawmill, right?" He pulls at his long white beard and laughs to himself. "After losing a game one time he, like, threw a fit and screamed at the umpire and stomped over to the little scoreboard and ripped off the panels used to keep score and rearranged them so that his team won. Then he said 'There!'"

He chuckles to himself.

"You should have heard the guy. 'There!' Triumphant and pouty at the same time. Magnificent."

He swivels and looks up at Mr. Andrews who is standing to the left of his desk. "Could you imagine living with that guy? Could you imagine being *married* to that fucking guy? Going on vacation with that guy? Goddamn…" he shakes his head, mystified. "I don't doubt for a second that his kid is a nightmare. You know who you should talk to?" He clears some space on his desk and writes a name on a post-it note. "Ted Downey over in the middle school. I play in a blues band with him, real good guy. I remember him going on about Mason Graham a few years ago." He hands him the note and reclines heavily in his chair. "Don't get him too riled up."

The next day, Mr. Andrews walks across the football and baseball fields and goes in the back entrance of the middle school. It is similar to the high school: dingy, bunker-like, water stains on the styrofoam-y ceiling tiles. He knocks on the open door of room 223 and peers inside. An enormous man stands with his back to the door. He has the body of a champion shot-putter thirty years past its prime. His hair is gray and thick. He stands like military brass. He is hanging up Halloween decorations.

"Spooky season?" Mr. Andrews asks.

"It's always spooky season in middle school."

They sit down in two student desks facing one another.

"So, Mason Graham strikes again."

"What can you tell me about him?"

"He's a psychopath."

Mr. Andrews nods as if to say "go on."

"An actual psychopath. Probably some kind of narcissistic personality disorder too, but an out-and-out psychopath."

"What makes you say that?"

"He tortures people. You've seen how the other kids are around him. He's an expert manipulator. Lies for the thrill of it. You know. You can just *feel* it when you talk to him."

"He's cruel," he says, "there's no doubt about that. But a psychopath?"

Mr. Downey nods absently and sucks his teeth. "Do you know how many psychopaths are in the world?"

Mr. Andrews is slow to shake his head.

"About one in one hundred. Generally. Globally. About one percent of the population is psychopathic."

"Then why don't I know more Mason Grahams?"

"You do. You've just never been vulnerable enough to be prey."

"How am I any more vulnerable now?"

He folds his python-sized arms. "You're new here? New to town?"

He nods.

"You're in Mason Graham's world, my man."

"He's a child."

"He's spawn."

Their eye contact vibrates contentiously.

"My dad worked at the sawmill for most of his life. Back when Mason's grandfather ran the place. This is still a logging town, but back then, that was all there was. Everyone worked for the mill. Workers were getting maimed and mangled and chewed up, so they went on strike. I was six or seven maybe. It went on long enough that we went hungry. My old man would come home soaking wet after twelve hours on the picket line. Then we got an eviction notice. So did most of the town. Because guess who owned — guess who still owns — the low rent housing around here? The trailer parks and the little Hooverville subdivisions? And then the strike was over. Just like that. Foster Graham hosted a company picnic in Graham Park to celebrate. I remember him making some kind of speech from the bandstand. He had this horrible grin. This nauseating, smug, self-satisfied grin. And I'll tell you what," he says, shifting uncomfortably in his seat, his throat tightening, "I damn near shit myself when I saw that exact same fucking grin in my classroom fifty years later."

Mr. Andrews watches as Mr. Downey's giant lungs heave with therapy-inspired deep breaths.

"Evil is just power exercised," he finally says. "And here, in this town, the Grahams have all the power."

Mr. Andrews broaches his counter cautiously. "You don't think that maybe his behavior is connection-seeking? Maybe he just needs a positive role model? He's still young. He can still be saved."

"Saved?" There is a hint of disgust in his voice. He takes a breath and looks up and away. "Saved from what?"

Mr. Andrews studies the colossal man in front of him whose face is now contorted in pained confusion.

"Look," he says, the tension loosening. "You seem like a nice guy. Don't do this to yourself. Let him win. For God's sake, just let him win. It's not worth it. Give him what he wants so you can at least be more present for your other students."

He thanks Mr. Downey for his time, who does not rise to see him out. As he walks down the hallway he hears the old teacher, distant like a conscience, plead: "Let him win."

The next day Mason introduces the laser pointer.

"Give me the laser pointer," Mr. Andrews says, holding out his hand.

Mason stares up at him, grinning viciously.

"Give me the laser pointer, Mason."

He puts the laser pointer back into his pocket. "What laser pointer?"

"Mason, I'm serious. Give me the laser pointer."

Mason waits a beat, and then: "I'm done. I'm sorry. I won't do it again."

Mr. Andrews stands with his hand out a moment longer, but Mason doesn't budge. He decides to let it go — escalating only ever works in Mason's favor.

When he sees the red dot once again circling his crotch, he strides towards Mason, an unfamiliar heat flooding the banks of his nervous system. The boy, laughing uproariously, keeps the laser point trained below Mr. Andrews' belt buckle.

He deftly snatches the laser pointer as Mason fails to recoil in time. The laughing stops abruptly, frighteningly. The boy leaps out of his seat and shouts with vein-throbbing, unhinged fury "That's my property! You stole my property! I'll call the police!"

"I am not stealing it," Mr. Andrews says through his teeth. "I am confiscating it. You can have it back at the end of the day."

"You're a thief! You can't steal my property! I have rights! I have my fourth amendment right! You need a warrant to seize my property!"

"Mason, this is so unacceptable," he says, projecting his voice with stormy affect. "I do not get spoken to like that in my classroom. In the hallway. Immediately."

"Mason," he says to the smirking child in the hallway. The boy ambles in loose circles with his hands behind his back, looking about him as if perusing a museum. "Mason," he says again. "We need to figure this out."

"Figure what out?"

"Whatever *this* is."

Still the boy floats around the hallway with his chin up.

"You have mistaken my kindness for weakness for the last time. I am your teacher and you will respect me."

"Oh yeah?" He says, the "yeah" blended with a derisive laugh.

"Yes. Now show me some respect and look me in the eye when I talk to you."

The boy snaps to attention and lunges into Mr. Andrews' personal space, making horrible, hateful eye contact only inches from his teacher's face. Mr. Andrews holds his ground.

"Has anyone ever told you you look like Ned Flanders? Like, if Ned Flanders shaved his mustache and was a total closet case, he'd be you."

"What makes you think you can talk to a teacher like that?"

"Do you say shit 'howdilydoodily'? Do you have little 'live love laugh' pillows on your couch? I'll bet you do."

"That is so unacceptable, Mason. Do you talk to other adults like this?"

"Did you get kicked out of all the bathhouses in Portland? Is that why you came down here? Or did your little Catholic school fire you when they found out you like getting railed up the —"

"That's enough!"

"That's enough," he repeats in a tone even more nasally than normal.

"Are you… copying me?"

He snarls fiercely: "Are you copying me?"

Mr. Andrews backs away. He beholds what is in front of him and realizes with horror that he does not recognize it. He has never seen it before. A grin spreads across the boy's face, and Mr. Andrews feels for a second that the creature in front of him is not human. He shivers.

"Back to class," he says as he returns to the room.

Behind him he hears, in a puerile voice: "you have mistaken my kindness for weakness."

Principal Driscoll does not respond to Mr. Andrews' email. This is not unexpected.

After all the students clear the building, he makes his way to her office. She is sitting pushed back from her desk, scrolling on her phone.

"Principal Driscoll," he says, drawing her attention from her phone.

"Mr. Andrews," she says. "Come in. Have a seat."

"I was hoping I could talk to you about a student I'm having trouble with."

"Mason Graham?"

"Yes, actually. How did you know?"

"I just got off the phone with his mother."

"Is that so?"

"She says he's terrified of you. Says you screamed at him in front of the whole class."

"I have never screamed at a student."

"Apparently he's been having terrible anxiety about going to your class. He came in here during lunch today almost in tears. We had to bring his food to him in the nurse's office."

Mr. Andrews' chin recedes into his neck, his eyebrows furrow incredulously. He tries to process all of this, but his mind's eye has been hijacked by the image of the principal feeding grapes to a toga-clad Mason while he lounges in the sick bed.

"That is certainly not how he presents in class."

They each wait for the other to speak.

"We take our students' mental health very seriously here."

"Of course."

A clock ticks thunderously above the principal's head.

"I know you're coming from a Catholic school, but the whole reign-of-terror thing is not going to fly here."

"I think you're misunderstanding —"

She raises her voice and plows right over Mr. Andrews' protestations.

"I'm not misunderstanding anything. Mason is one of our best students. Having a laser pointer in class is not a good reason to terrify a sweet, sensitive boy like Mason. His parents will be here in ten minutes to meet with us."

"Ten minutes?" he says. "You are giving me ten minutes notice on a parent meeting?"

"You can have a seat at the conference table."

Mr. Andrews hears the sharp thuds of approaching cowboy boots from beyond the door. They grow louder, like his heartbeats, and stop briefly, uncomfortably, before entering. In walk Mason, his mother, and a bullnecked man in an emerald green U of O hoodie and a cowboy hat. Mr. Andrews stands up and extends his hand across the conference table but is ignored. The Grahams, all three of them, sit across the table from him. Ms. Driscoll alone remains standing. Mason's dad, Linus Graham, glares at Mr. Andrews with a menacing scowl. He has the same round face and sharp chin and maggot-colored complexion as his son. The same wide-set eyes and the same arrogant gravitas.

"What's this I hear about you threatening my son?"

"Excuse me?" Mr. Andrews is indignant, outraged. He looks to Mason who catches his eye and smirks deviously. "I have never threatened a student."

Mason's mother, a tall, gaunt woman whose eyes seem to forever gaze vacantly at some distant, hopeless catastrophe says, "Go on, baby. Tell us what happened."

Mason looks sheepishly at the floor and twists his toe in the carpet.

"Mr. Andrews called me into the hallway and said... I was going to respect him... or else."

"Or else!" Linus shouts. "Or else, what?"

Mr. Andrews waits patiently for the words to stick their landing. He turns slowly to Principal Driscoll who, with arms folded, judges disapprovingly from on high.

"This is preposterous," declares Mr. Andrews.

"Preposterous! Pre-posterous!" Linus shouts. "Who the fuck do you think you are coming in here talking like that? Talking to my boy like that."

"This has gone on long enough. Mason, come on. Let's be men about this."

"Then," Mason says dolefully, "he asked me... if I knew... what a bathhouse was."

The mother gasps and covers her mouth with her hands.

"You call my son a queer! You try to turn my son into a *queer*!"

"This is outrageous. I have never —"

"Now you're calling my son a liar!"

"Your son needs to be held accountable —"

"How fucking dare you. How fucking dare you," he says before launching into a deafening homophobic tirade that Mr. Andrews scarcely hears. His mind is elsewhere, on a rainy winter night in the 1890s. In front of him is Mason Graham on horseback, wearing a leather duster and wilting cowboy hat, the steam erupting from his mouth as he points at every tree he passes and barks: "Mine! Mine! Mine!"

"I want answers! I want to know who hired this fucking twink in the first place!"

Only now does Ms. Driscoll step in. "I'm terribly sorry, Mr. Graham. Terribly sorry. This is all so embarrassing. I'll personally see to it that Mr. Andrews is disciplined appropriately."

"Absolutely goddamn right," he says.

"Mr. Andrews," Ms. Driscoll asks, "do you have anything to say for yourself?"

He pauses and considers the question seriously, but again finds himself leering at Mason, at the scurrilous grin now stretching from ear to ear. He shakes his head. "No."

The Graham family rises. As Linus reaches for the door, Mason turns around.

"I sure hope we can turn over a new leaf, Mr. Andrews. I really do enjoy being in your class."

The door shuts and the thudding boot heels recede until they are subsumed by the clock's second hand.

"We will have a formal discipline hearing tomorrow after school," she says to him. "Don't bother trying to get the union involved."

He looks at her, disgusted. "I don't think so." He threads the brass key off its lanyard and tosses it on the conference table as he stands up.

Without another word, he leaves her office and returns to his classroom to pack up his belongings. Awaiting him on his desk are a laser pointer and a four-by-two inch portrait of St. Ignatius, whose stern countenance gazes past him, through him, at the evergreens beyond his window. They are alive with quarrelsome birds who flit and squawk in the late afternoon light. To Mr. Andrews, though, it sounds for all the world as if even the trees are laughing at him.

Endoscopy

I'd been careful, exceedingly careful; I'd scarcely left my house since March. I wore gloves and not one — but two! — masks whenever I was forced to brave the surface world. Am I scared of coronavirus? Yes. I am not a lucky man, you see. I would surely be one of the poor fuckers with ghastly long term ailments, condemned to shuffle around breathless and confused and miserable for decades to come. I saw such a fate expand before me the day my esophagus started to hurt. And it was made all the worse knowing how I'd contracted the virus. The fact that I'd been infected by inhaling a cloud of steamy vapor that had already been inside of some slovenly wretch's body. Inside somebody's nose and lungs and mouth, mingling with their snots and nose hairs and spit and the fetid shit that lives between their unbrushed teeth. Goddamn foul is what it is. Goddamn violating. And there was only one place where I could have gotten it. Let me tell you what happened.

I'd gone to Target, you see. The one in East Tucson at the end of 22nd street. I was in need of toilet paper, you see, but it had been two months and there was still no toilet paper to be found.

I stood in the aisle and ground my teeth as I glared at the off-white, hole-punched metal shelves. Out there somewhere were hundreds, thousands of people with closets full of toilet paper. So much toilet paper that they were using it to make obstacle courses for their cats. Using it for art projects and party streamers and mummy costumes. While there I was, humbly seeking only a six pack. A four-pack! A single individually wrapped roll!

At the end of the aisle just around the corner I heard some commotion. The sound of thin plastic wrapping crunching like dry leaves. Could it be? I hurried over and saw a man pushing a cart full of toilet paper. The surrounding shelves were empty. He must have just unloaded them, pushed them all off in one fell swoop. He was large, intimidating even, with broad features and simian forearms. He was possessed of a creepy old man strength, and he was hairy and leathery in a Mediterranean way. He had a stubbly scowl where a mask should have been.

"Excuse me," I said. I was so polite, see how polite I was? "Excuse me, other people need toilet paper, too."

There was an unhinged bewilderment on his face.

"I worked in the sun for forty fucking years," he said with a venomous drawl. "I don't have to listen to a little chicken shit like you."

"The least you could do is give me one pack. You can't spare one pack?"

He lumbered over to me in one or two steps and got right in my face. He shouted:

"Why would anyone give a fuck about *you*?"

Right in my face, mind you. Really gave me a good spritzing with that percussive "fuck." I had to clean my glasses, to give you an idea. He lurched past me, rammed my cart with a puerile "hmmpf" and resumed stalking the aisles.

I ruminated bitterly on that encounter for days, indulging in the most gruesome of revenge fantasies and wishing an agonizing and protracted death on that Sasquatch. When I woke up a few days later with my esophagus all inflamed and buzzing, I shouted and thrashed in my bed. I called my doctor and demanded — demanded! — a coronavirus test. They were in short supply, he said, but it was goddamn urgent, I said! And I'd already been dismissed and walked all over enough! He sighed and relented, and you can be sure he shoved that extra long cotton swab all the way up my nose that very day.

"You're sure it's negative?" I asked my doctor during a tele-med follow-up.

"Yes, Gordon," he said, "You don't have coronavirus."

"But are you sure? Couldn't it be a false negative? Or maybe they mixed up my test with someone else?"

"That is exceedingly unlikely, Gordon. And given that you haven't developed any symptoms, I think you're in the clear."

"But what about the pain in my chest?" I was losing patience, and justifiably so! "My esophagus has been on fire for almost two weeks!"

"It's most likely just heartburn. This has been a very stressful episode for you, I'm sure."

"It's not heartburn! I know what heartburn feels like!"

"Go to Walgreens and pick up some Prilosec. We can follow up in three weeks."

"Prilosec! Three weeks! I need an endoscopy. I need a referral to a gastroenterologist."

"I can't do that, Gordon. Try the Prilosec, and if it really doesn't work we can reassess in three weeks."

"But —"

"I have another patient, Gordon. You can schedule a follow-up online. Take care."

The video chat ended abruptly and I gnashed my teeth in impotent fury. So quick was he to dismiss my suffering as some triviality. In three weeks they'd declare me terminal and say, "Alas! If only we'd caught it sooner!" And then everyone would know that it wasn't just heartburn. Everyone would know that my suffering was legitimate. And my final joy in this world would be to see the regret on that doctor's face as he realized that his disregard for my pain was the final nail in my coffin.

Obviously the Prilosec didn't work. After ten days on this preposterous drug trial it became clear that the pain in my esophagus was not going anywhere. It hurt. All the time. Not like heartburn. It was not heartburn. It felt like I swallowed a thistle, or a stinging nettle, or a jellyfish. A weird buzzing sort of pain. And I had trouble swallowing. Not specifically food, but just swallowing in general. Sometimes I could feel an obstruction. I could feel whatever I swallowed squeeze past a budding tumor, black and spidery, clinging to the soft pinkness of my esophagus like some ghoulish deer tick draining the life out of me. I could damn near feel it pulsate with each slurp. There was no respite. Not at night, not when I watched TV, not when I drank cold water. Nothing soothed it, and nothing could distract me from it. I was left to fidget and pace like a flea-bitten dog. Though I'd initially reveled in the lockdown, the walls of my little East Tucson bungalow were becoming downright sepulchral.

Working from home, too, was initially enjoyable. No longer was I subject to the mind-numbing idiocy of water cooler talk and morning sales briefings. No more feigned enthusiasm for people's babies or new RVs or stupid fucking ski trips. No more rush hour road rage. I could fill out spreadsheets and index expense reports from the comfort of my couch.

Sadly, that was not to last.

My boss was a power-suit, middle management type who ran a tight ship. When she requested a Zoom session, I figured it was for a rundown of quarterly numbers. But no.

"Gordon, we need to have a conversation about your performance."

"My performance? There is nothing wrong with my performance."

"It's becoming increasingly clear that —"

"I get my work done. I crunch the numbers that need to be crunched. What else do you want from me?"

"Gordon, your participation since working remotely has been subpar."

"Participation? Is this middle school?"

"I've been clear that you cannot make your own hours."

"And why not?"

"That's not the conversation we're having."

"Like I said, I get my work done. What does it matter to you when I do it?"

"This business is a team effort, Gordon. You have to actually work with other people to—"

"Oh, please. You just want another yes man. Well I'm no yes man."

"No one's denying that." She leaned back and took a breath. "Look, Gordon. As far as I'm concerned, you're showing up an hour late and leaving an hour early every day. You could at least turn on your camera during morning meetings. You don't get special treatment just because—"

"I am dealing with a medical problem, I'll have you know! Chronic pain, in fact! How many times do I have to tell you? Why does no one care? I have been a diligent employee for 15 years and I am suffering here and no one cares!"

"Gordon, this has been hard on all of us, and you need to recognize that you're not the only—"

"Unbelievable. Unbelievable! How is it that you can't extend any sympathy to me during—"

"Look, Gordon. Here's the deal." She took off her glasses and pinched the bridge of her nose. "We're losing money. Fast. Upper management is demanding cuts and I'm letting you go."

"What!" There was no moment of stunned silence; my volley was swift and forceful. "You can't do that to me! I've been at this company for years, *years* —"

"Yes, and you have been rude and unpleasant for every one of them —"

"You're firing *me*? Who will run the accounting office? Dieter? That man is a buffoon, he—"

"Gordon," she said. "Shut up," she said. "Please just shut up. You shared a cubicle with Dieter for, what, seven years? I can't believe you would try to throw him under the bus like that."

"Dieter is a fucking moron and I deserve—"

She threw her hands up in frustration. "You are unbelievable," she said. "God, you are pathetic. You know HR literally has a file of complaints against you? And if it wasn't for Dieter you would have been fired years ago. I would have done it myself but Dieter went to bat for you so many times, and I haven't the slightest idea why."

"You don't even have the authority to fire me!"

"Ha!" She laughed sharply. "This meeting is over. You're finished. You'll be locked out of your account and your email tonight. Your insurance benefits will terminate at the end of the month. Goodbye, Gordon."

"Wait, the end of the—"

But she was gone.

Now was the time for stunned silence. Before contemplating the loss of income or the insufferable job search ahead of me, I grappled with the fact that the month would be over in four days. Then it would be June, and I would be a pauper with the most plebeian of health insurance plans, and I would be forced to get an endoscopy in a veterinary clinic south of the border. How could they do this to me! Cast me out like this in my time of strife!

Swift action was in order; I had to move my follow up appointment to the next day and squeak it in under my current plan (I'd already met my deductible, you see).

I hunted for my phone and scrolled through my contacts. I paced nervously and grimaced in a sour, scrunched-up sort of way as I listened to the infernal recorded options menu. Then came the call-waiting music, infuriatingly out of synch with the second hand ticking its way toward closing time.

"Southwest Allied Physicians, Dr. Torres' office. This is Larissa speaking."

"Hi! Yes!" I hollered with a red-faced intensity. "This is Gordon Keller. I need to reschedule an appointment."

"Oh," she said. "Hi, Mr. Keller," she said. "Dr. Torres is pretty booked…"

"Oh, come on," I said. "This is urgent. This is of the most extreme urgency! I need to move my appointment up to some-time this week."

"Mmm," she said as she feigned clicking through a calendar. "Sorry, Dr. Torres is all booked for the rest of the week."

"No, damn you! How am I not a preferred patient at this point?"

She sighed heavily. "That's really not how this works, Mr. Keller."

"Well, it should!"

"Well, it doesn't. Dr. Torres has many patients with needs as urgent as your own. The soonest I could reschedule you is the second week of June. Would you like to cancel your appoint-ment on the 4th?"

I held the phone away to indulge the pressure building in my head.

"Mr. Keller?"

"No," I said through gritted teeth. "No, don't cancel the appointment."

"Ok. You'll have a Zoom link sent to your email on file."

I hung up and flopped on the couch. Then I screamed into a pillow. I'm not sure why I bothered with the pillow; there wasn't a soul around to hear me anyway.

The summer heat plateaued. I was mired in a despair so deep, so intractable, that I could barely function. I spent many hours just sitting on my couch. I gave up looking for another job. I would say I stared at the wall, but "stare" feels too active of a verb. The space in front of me existed unobserved, my full attention devoted to the towering inferno that was my interior life. The pain in my chest was staggering. Indefatigable is the only word for it; it never waned or dissipated or weakened. It was ever-present, mechanical in its alertness. It felt almost as if it was stalking me. Like the pain itself was hiding in the shadows, intensely assessing me with unblinking eyes. Sharp, yellow eyes. Like the eyes of a jaguar. Or a snake. And I couldn't quite tell what was going on behind those eyes. Was it eager to pounce? Was it resisting a gnawing hunger, waiting eagerly for a preordained time? I could not escape it anymore than one can escape the feeling of being watched. Nothing could distract me long enough to ever feel at ease.

I managed to sign myself up for some government health care, but it was effectively useless — a seven thousand dollar deductible and 14,000 out of pocket max. I would be paying for the endoscopy myself, but so be it!

The follow-up appointment was not as straightforward as I'd hoped.

"I'll write you a prescription for some higher dose Omeprazole," he said. "That should reduce your stomach acid over time and help with the heartburn."

"For the last time," I said, "It isn't heartburn. There is something gravely wrong with my esophagus. This is no run-of-the-mill discomfort!"

"Gordon," he sighed. "I think this is just like what we went through last November with your prostate. Or that time you thought you had a stomach parasite. Or that thing with your heart—"

"No!" I slammed the table with enough force to shift my webcam. "Those episodes are in no way analogous to—"

"Gordon, please," he said. "I'm not denying that the pain you're experiencing is real. I don't doubt that you are hurting. I just don't think it has a physical origin."

"How the hell could you know that? How dare you accuse me of imagining this!"

"Psychosomatic pain is not imaginary. In fact, it is not an unreasonable response to such unprecedented times."

"You think I just want attention? You think I'm out here paying out of pocket just so I can have your undivided attention?"

"I think you want validation."

"What the fuck does that mean?"

"I think you need someone to confirm that your pain — and I'm not talking about the pain in your chest — is real. You want something to be wrong with you so that—"

"Unbelievable! You goddamn quack! What is this? I want to be sick? I want to have this agony in my chest? Like I want your pity? I should report you! I'll report this quackery to the relevant authorities!"

"Gordon..."

"No. You listen to me. I want a referral for an endoscopy. You are my healthcare provider, which means you are required to provide me with healthcare, not feel-good snowflake bullshit."

"Fine." He leaned back in his chair. "Fine. I'll refer to you Dr. Mijani. He's a gastroenterologist. I advise you take a more respectful tone with him."

"Thank you," I said, exasperated. Now was that so hard, I wanted to say.

"Goodbye, Gordon. Good luck with all this."

I ended the call there. No doubt that charlatan was charging me by the minute. But I got what I wanted, what I needed! The bill came in at 375 dollars for that nonsense, but by God I was finally on my way to getting some answers. I would finally know what was to blame for my agony. I would have something to show for my pain, something to point to, a diagnosis to condense my nebulous suffering into something tangible, a little VIP pass that no one could ignore.

The waiting game began in earnest after that tele-med snake oil clownery. The soonest appointment I could get with this Mijani character wasn't until July. July! He must be going on vacation, I said! Taking half-days now and then, I said! And this only for a consultation! The receptionist paid no heed. I had time to kill, so long as time didn't kill me first.

The pandemic was raging and a wildfire was burning out of control in the mountains north of town. The air was thick with carcinogens and viral loads, all looking to colonize my soft, unsuspecting lungs. I scarcely left my house. I had little reason to, save for the odd grocery run. The heat was goddamn oppressive. It was offensive to my esophagus; the dry air aggravated the charred tube of flesh in my chest. I emerged only in the mornings and at night like some shifty-eyed desert dweller poking its snout out of its burrow. I never strayed beyond my stoop. How could I! The heat could cause the monstrosity in my chest to hemorrhage, or I could just have an aneurysm and croak right there on the street. I'd just eat it face first and my skin would instantly fuse to the blacktop and the paramedics would have to peel me off like a recalcitrant price tag. They'd probably just grab me by the hair, give me a sharp tug, and leave a ghoulish inversion of my face smiling back up at them.

How did I spend my days, you ask? The truth is that I stopped making sense of my life in linear, narrative terms. There was no beginning, middle, or end to my days anymore. Chronic pain has a way of distorting time. The intensity is damning enough, but it is the persistence that really does it. The notion that it would not stop, that it might never stop, that it will hurt *forever*, is perhaps the truest torture that exists. The vastness of "forever" triggered a kind of agoraphobic panic; the prospect of 20, 40, 60 more years — cosmic, inconceivable expanses of time to feel this way — warped time to the scale of geologic eras.

My nights were no better. I didn't sleep for weeks, you see. Not well, at least. I drifted off every now and then, but it was fractured enough to create the illusion of endless tossing and turning. I speculated endlessly on the origin of my pain, and I'd scroll through a demented Instagram of my own curating, post after maudlin post of my impending death.

The pain infiltrated my dreams, too. They started off nebulous, but as the walls of the dreamscape came into focus and my subconscious condensed into avatars and archetypes, the pain seeped in. It was not like in waking life where the pain was internal; in these dreams the pain was somehow ambient. Like heat. Like wifi. Just *there*, written into the source code of the dream. It was vague at first, as if distant, but it approached with the steadiness of a drumbeat, like a foreign army marching just beyond the hills.

Sometimes it took its time, letting entire narratives unfold before overtaking me. Though the pace varied, the pain was linear and merciless in its approach. And as the pain swelled, the dream became more lucid. The setting morphed to fit my panic; my projections decayed into hellish distortions of people and places I knew, and the tension built in concert with the pain. It rose like freezing seawater in the hull of a sinking ship until finally it came to my neck, my jaw. I'd hyperventilate and press my cheek against the steel ceiling and kiss the air with frenzied final breaths.

And then I'd wake up. Just before the pain swallowed me whole.

I took to perusing WebMD. Yes, yes, I know it was a bad idea. But fuck you, I needed answers. At least WebMD didn't make me wait four weeks just to tell me it could be anything. It turns out that a robot doctor was just as concerned with the nuances of my suffering as the human one. I finally saw the gastroenter-ologist, you see, and he wasn't in the least bit interested in my condition. Not even in an abstract intellectual way.

The office was in a grungy part of town, ugly even by Tucson standards. The waiting room was full to the brim with dozens of saggy, drooping people so exhausted by their misery that it was all they could do to shuffle and slouch through life as if in line for something vague and only dimly remembered.

I was racked with this knee-bouncing anxiety that I wouldn't hear the nurse call my name above the din of people's groans and rumbling stomachs and I would just wait around this foul limbo until closing time.

"Just wanted to check on the status of things," I said to the receptionist after my appointment time had long passed.

"Dr. Mijani is running a little late today," she said without looking up at me. "It will be just a minute."

"I just wanted to make sure I didn't miss my name being called or—"

"I doubt that very much, sir."

After nearly forty minutes a nurse led me to what I suspected was formerly a storage closet. An off-center poster detailing the digestive tract decorated the wall. It felt like a cynical, half-assed attempt to make the room into something more than just an empty space. I studied it regardless and was suddenly struck by the revelation that all my internal workings carried on in the dark. An inky, abyssal darkness. A tangible darkness, neither solid nor liquid, but fluid and rich. Capital-N Nothing, that's what it was. That's what was feasting on me, trapped inside me like a djinn in a lamp, clawing its way up my esophagus, desperate to escape and, in turn, swallow me in poetic revenge.

The doctor blew into the room like a door-busting draft and sat some ten feet away from me. He was a rotund man who had the air of someone who dismissed others with a flick of his wrist. He seemed sleepy and bored, and he flipped through some papers while I launched into the spiel I'd been rehearsing in my head for six weeks. He listened to none of it, and then asked me if I'd ever had an endoscopy before. I said no, and he rose from his chair.

"I'll have my assistant schedule one," he said, making for the door.

"Wait, but what do you think is wrong with me?" I blurted out as he pulled the door open.

"Could be anything." Though he faced me, I got the sense that he wasn't really looking at me. "Probably acid reflux. Maybe an allergy. Impossible to say without having a look. My assistant will be in to schedule you."

He was long gone before I could sputter out any follow ups.

I was crestfallen, truly. I'd anticipated this moment for so long, spent so many hours on my couch envisioning the tense Aaron Sorkin dialogue we'd exchange as the doctor and I got to the bottom of an enthralling medical mystery.

But indeed, he didn't care. My suffering was unremarkable to him, utterly pedestrian. So much so, in fact, that his assistant returned only to tell me that it could wait.

"Five weeks!" My outrage was more panicked than indignant. I damn near leapt out of the chair. "You don't understand,

I could be dead in five weeks. I can't wait five weeks. Please, I can't wait five weeks."

"That is the earliest we are able to schedule you."

"I don't believe you!"

"Excuse me?"

"You're lying to me!"

"Sir, please calm down."

"You could schedule me sooner if you wanted to. If my life mattered to you one goddamn bit you'd find an open slot no problem."

"Sir, there are a lot of people who need endoscopies. If you feel like your life is in danger, you need to call 911."

She looked at me, but not with pity or ire. Just patient alertness. I could feel my glare soften and I sank back into the chair.

"Here are the instructions for the day of your procedure and directions to the clinic. You will need to have someone check you in and out of the appointment." She dropped a packet of papers on the desk by the door and left promptly.

I sat there, stunned and maybe on the verge of tears, but also unsure if there was more — if I was supposed to be waiting for something. I soon realized that no one was coming back.

It wasn't until later in the evening that I'd calmed down enough to think about what the doctor had actually said. He was wrong about the acid reflux. But the allergies. Maybe he was onto something. Maybe there was something in my life that was slowly poisoning me. Some mysterious, invisible allergen, hiding in plain sight. It could be in the air. It could be in my food.

I felt suddenly unclean. Contaminated. What if my life was so saturated with a toxin that it was in my clothes, on my toothbrush, in my sheets? I had nowhere to go, trapped forever in my house with this invisible, ambient threat and no way to defend myself.

I turned to the internet for some guidance. Indeed, there were a million things I could be allergic to, and suddenly developing allergies is not unheard of. I reviewed my daily intake of food. It could be anything. It could be wheat or corn or oats or soy. It could be some obscure synthetic additive.

But it might not be food. The internet assured me that it could be *anything*. Apparently cockroach feces is highly allergenic. A secretive roach lair could be writhing in my walls, in the vents, their tiny turds dispersed with my air conditioning. Smaller still, it could be dust mites, the little arachnids that feed on dead skin. Google them, I dare you. They creep on eight stubby legs and graze like herds of buffalo on the detritus of your eroding body, eager to consume you one dead cell at a time.

Or what if it was in the water? What if my pipes were slowly corroding and little shards of metal passed down my gullet with each swig, a swarm of microscopic batarangs eviscerating my esophagus and intestines.

Could it be coming from outside? Is there some wicked desert flora dispersing noxious pollen at all hours? Or could there be something seeping up from the ground, perhaps the chem trails of the insecticide the landlord sprays? Or maybe the paint on my walls was degrading and leaching into the air and settling on my pillow like dandruff?

I felt suddenly that there is no emptiness in this world; every square inch of space is saturated with agents of suffering all lingering like ticks on a blade of grass, just waiting for me to walk by so that they can pounce and pierce my all-too porous being.

I began to panic, hyperventilate. I paced back and forth feeling like the ground might just split open beneath me and swallow me whole, absorb me into the terra-cotta tiles and shed my essence from the walls.

I lowered all the windows, shut all the blinds. I turned off the AC to keep it from spewing any filth. I put two masks on and began to scrub my house vigorously, liberally applying the Lysol until I realized I was only adding to the toxic fog I inhabited.

I unpacked a long-stowed sleeping bag and crawled into it, no longer trusting my sheets. It had been sealed in its sack for so long that surely it was safe. I pulled up the hood and cinched the drawstrings tight. I curled up tighter still, burrowing deep into the darkness of my cocoon.

All told, I spent about 14 hours in the sleeping bag. I woke up with a vacant sort of feeling not unlike a brutal caffeine comedown. The anxiety shrank back into its den during the night, but that morning I could still hear its jagged Jabberwocky claw rapping against the inside of my skull.

I had to cut my losses. The AC could not stay off — the desert heat would kill me faster than any hypothetical mystery spores. I drank water only from gallon jugs purchased at the store. I limited my diet to oatmeal, crackers, rice, and cabbage. Did I wear a mask around my house? Yes. It was a crisis of trust, you see. Every molecule was out to get me, existence itself was a universal solvent intent on absorbing me, digesting me. I was but a tootsie pop in the mouth of some cosmic beast, each caustic lick eroding me into oblivion.

And so it went for five more weeks.

I spent about half an hour on hold with the hospital. There was a phone number on the info packet I'd received at Dr. Mijani's office for pre-procedure inquiries. It was only days away, and, well, I was in a bind. A young nurse or administrative assistant of some kind finally picked up.

"How serious is this chaperone thing?"

"We won't perform the procedure if you don't have a responsible adult on hand for you."

"But it's just to make sure that I don't drive, right? You just can't let me drive after the anesthetic. Can't I just take a cab?"

"No, no cabs or ubers. It's a liability thing. And in case there is a complication or emergency."

"Well, what if I don't have anyone to take me?"

There was a moment of hesitation on the other end. "You don't have any family or friends in the area who can check you in?"

"No, I…" my gaze drifted out the window. Nothing stirred in the midday heat, the irradiated, prickly excuse of a yard frightened me somehow. "No. No one."

"Have you reached out to any neighbors or colleagues?"

"I said no one, goddamnit!"

"If you're really in a pinch, you can sign a medical release waiver and arrange a medical transport. It doesn't look like your insurance will cover it, though"

"Send it to my email on file," I said and hung up.

The night before the endoscopy I couldn't sleep. They make you fast from food and water for a full twelve hours, and I was predictably anxious to finally know my nemesis. I would have no one to take care of me upon returning home, so I decided to stock up on water and Tylenol rather than toss and turn in bed.

I found the store deserted. I'd already gathered most of my essentials when I realized they'd shut off the muzak that usually fills the space. In its place was the fluorescent buzz of the refrigerators and lights. Though it had been haunting me unnoticed, the moment I heard it I was paralyzed. It sounded, somehow, like the pain in my chest. I gazed vacantly at the floor as the buzzing grew louder and louder, reverberating in my head and finding resonance with the electric tingling in my esophagus.

I came to my senses and rushed outside, abandoning my half-filled cart in the middle of the freezer section. But even in the parking lot, that shrill buzz awaited me, emanating from the moth-covered lights that shone down on me so brutally.

I drove home with that buzz still in my head, still in my chest. Static gushed through the radio when I turned it on. The streets and intersections were downright lunar in their emptiness. I ran a red light, so eager was I to burrow back into my hovel and hide. But there was no hiding from this — it was everywhere, it was inside me. It buzzed like a fly-covered carcass, like a motel vacancy sign, like some ravenous, many-bladed machine. It was the background frequency of my cavernous headspace. It was tinnitus of the soul. It was the seething growl of that shadowy, amorphous djinn.

There was no peace in returning home. I felt, strangely, as if I was trespassing. Without turning on the lights, I looked around and saw my life as a stranger or a burglar might. All my familiar possessions were suddenly inert objects that meant nothing to no one, mere props that served only to fill space and project some phony facsimile of a life.

I saw socks on the couch. Crumbs on the table. Dishes in the sink. A sleeping bag, deflated on my bed. It all smelled pungently of me.

I glanced at myself sidelong in the mirror. I was ghastly pale in the moonlight, and as I glided slowly toward myself, a vision of my corpse emerged from the dark. I reached out hoping that the glass would ripple and bend and I would wake up with a start. But no. My eyes seemed to be retreating into my skull, cravenly scanning the world from a distance. My spidery hands, all knuckle and vein, crept across my cheekbones and traced the delicate ridge of my orbital. I pulled off my shirt. My ribs embraced me like the chitinous shell of a parasitic alien. My arms dangled like a scarecrow's. My head looked too heavy for my neck.

I backed away and beheld my benthic loneliness. With tears in my eyes, I called the only person I thought might just pick up.

Dieter was on time to get me.

He brought the family van. It smelled vaguely of dog and McDonalds. Children's toys and the odd item of clothing littered the back. I'd always held a good deal of contempt for the guy. I found his workplace collegiality to be unctuous, his good humor to be an indicator of a soft mind. His doughy body had always vaguely disgusted me, and the wispy hair that covered his bald spot made me embarrassed for him. I scheduled my lunch break to maximize time apart. But this morning, as he sat twisted in the pilot seat of a disheveled minivan, his awkwardness was endearing, disarming even, and I found myself stammering on a jumbled greeting.

"Sorry about the mess," he said, nodding towards the back.

I was tongue-twisted in a jittery sort of way, and I folded my arms tightly as we pulled into the street. His phone was mounted on the dash. The screen was cracked in the corner. A calm robot voice gave directions through the convoluted streets of my neighborhood.

It's shaping up to be the hottest summer in Tucson history, he said. No monsoon this year, can you believe it, he said. Meanwhile, I did battle with a tangle of self-doubt and anxiety. Finally, I loosed myself enough to ask: Why?

"Why what?"

I was defensive even here, regretting my tone as I snapped at him. "Why help me? Why even pick up the phone? Why take an entire morning off work for me? I've never been kind to you."

He was silent for a moment.

"You know, Gordon," he said, "I always figured it must be really hard to be you."

I had a retort brewing but it got caught in my throat.

I hugged myself tighter and turned away from Dieter to look out the window with my whole body.

Dieter signed me in and wished me luck and left me to sit in the waiting room. I agreed to a monthly payment plan. I got my little plastic wristband.

A nurse stuck me with an IV and went to get the next patient. I felt a wave of dizziness, perhaps from the fast, perhaps not. I'd been so furiously rushing to this moment that upon coming to a sudden stop, the g-force of it all was overwhelming. All my anger and loneliness and fear crashed over me like the wake of some great ship, leaving me floundering and sputtering in a whirl of self-pity. I looked upon my own weakness for the first time with sorrow instead of revulsion and saw, finally, the tragedy of my delusional conviction that I am plagued by something more majestic than the ambient suffering of life itself.

They wheeled me into a dark room illumined by glowing screens and monitors. I was suddenly reminded of the fact that my insides had never before been seen, never before been exposed to light. I shivered. That menacing djinn will retreat from the light like roaches on a countertop, taking refuge in colder depths until it can flood me once more.

Someone rolled me onto my left side and I saw the endoscopy hose hanging from a hook. The pleated rubber tube housed a thin wire with a light at the end like the bioluminescent bobble of a deep sea angler fish. The anesthetist told me to take three deep breaths, and as the darkness seeped in from my periphery, I knew, with some certainty, that probe and search as they might, they would find only nothing.

Deep Storage

Kevin wakes before his alarm. Sort of. He opens his eyes weakly, but closes them again to return to his dream. He is at a carnival. It's crowded. It's muggy. Everything is illuminated by blinking fairy lights. There is a ferris wheel. He's just lost at the ring toss. And he's with someone. But wait a minute. This isn't just a carnival, this is Glenwood Days. And that's Ally Golden. And all this actually happened. And they're eating ice cream at one of those sticky high tables and he spills some on his shirt and Ally laughs and then he wakes up.

But again he resists the pull to consciousness and drags the dream into his waking life. Try as he might to burrow back into the warmth of his subconscious, the carnival recedes from his mind's eye, tugged like Wilson out to sea. But the feeling remains, and he won't open his eyes for fear that daylight might break the spell. As long as he doesn't look, he can believe what he feels — that Ally Golden is lying next to him.

The poor guy is in love, like wildly and feverishly in love, with Ally Golden. Like his heart is full of sonnets, all for her. Like he would launch a thousand ships to see her one more time.

But it's not an erotic thing. He's not savagely horny or something. There was nothing sexy about the carnival dream, and this has nothing to do with his dick.

It's overwhelming, deeply confusing even. He's never felt this way before. About anyone. And so he sits on the edge of his bed with his head in his hands, trying to square the ecstasy of her spectral presence with the agony of her corporeal absence.

The bed is empty. She is not here. She was never here.

But Kevin is here, alone, and maniacally in love with Ally Golden, a woman he has not seen, let alone thought about, in over ten years. A woman who he only ever knew as a girl, a high school classmate, a friend and confidant, but never a lover.

The experience has an out-of-body ring to it. His reflection looks vague in the mirror, and his morning shower feels distant, like rain in the night.

He knows that it is patently ridiculous to think he's in love with Ally Golden. It's laughable, really. It's been a full decade. 2010 would have been the last time they saw each other. The summer after graduating high school. But he doesn't care how crazy it sounds. He'd rather have these feelings than not.

He is overcome thinking about her, speculating, fantasizing even, about who she became. Does she live in the city? Is she successful? Does she like her job? Is she happy? Fulfilled? In love?

He hopes so.

He hopes that every good thing that could ever happen to anyone happens to her. His desire is not to have her, or hold her, or run away with her — what he wants more than anything is for her to be happy. If he never sees her again, so be it. As long as she is happy. As long as her life is vibrant and rich and full of joy.

He puts on a shirt and tie, but doesn't bother with real pants. He's got a Zoom meeting at 8, and it is 7:59, and he's been sitting on his bed, wrapped in a damp towel for an undefined amount of time. He opens his computer, but his hair is still wet and he can't find his glasses but whatever: It is seven months into the pandemic and Kevin is checked out. From work, and to a lesser extent, life in general. The isolation has whittled him hollow. The anxiety has burned all the oxygen out of his interior life, and as of late, he's stopped feeling very much at all.

But not today. Today, for the first time in months, he feels *good*. His gaze drifts above his laptop, and for the duration of the Zoom meeting he just stares out the window, thinking about Ally Golden. He decides to catalog every memory he has of her.

They met in 8th grade in English class. They were assigned to do a group project on Dr. Jekyll and Mr. Hyde.

Freshman year, she asked him to winter formal. He was standing at his locker at the end of the day and she just came up and asked him real business-like and he was so goddamn awkward and surprised but he said yeah and was so nervous about it for the rest of the month that he almost bailed at the last second, but his mom made him go.

They were lab partners in chemistry class for a while, and she let him copy her notes.

They went mini-golfing once.

She ran for student council one year and put up these hilarious Dwight Schrute-themed campaign posters. She was really funny. He'd forgotten that about her. Like, she was really witty and laughed a lot.

One night he went over to her house to watch a movie, but no one else showed up. They watched *The Men Who Stare at Goats.*

He drove her home from somewhere one night and he showed her Explosions in the Sky. She said she'd never heard anything like it before. He parked outside her house and they just listened to it for a while in the dark.

And then there was the carnival.

But is that it? Is that really all the memories he can scrape together? All of these had been in deep storage, gathering dust somewhere in the rows of filing cabinets of his subconscious. Surely there are others. Little interactions in the hallway, laughs shared in the lunchroom, awkward high school social scenes. Were they gone for good? Were they ever even encoded? If he can't remember them, if they are locked in deep storage, do they still affect him? His personality? Or is it like they never happened?

All day he resists the sneaking urge to scour Ally's Facebook. He deactivated his account years ago, but he could theoretically spin it back up again. Just to send her a message, though. Not to creep on her or whatever.

So he does it. He signs back in and all of it is still there. All his tagged photos, his friends, etc. He doesn't look at any of it though. In fact, he makes a big deal, internally, about not looking at it, because he's scared he might come across a cringe picture of himself and relive some teenage mortification.

He drafts a message, but then deletes it. He does this several times over the course of the afternoon, some expanding into stream of consciousness essays which he knows better than to ever let anyone see. He finally lands on something short and breezy.

"Hey Ally, I caught myself thinking about you the other day. Hope you're hanging in there. Let me know if you'd like to reconnect."

He leaves his phone number at the end and hovers over the send button.

He rereads the lines compulsively and begins to freak out. The message had made it all too real — he'd made his fantasy manifest by roping the real life Ally Golden into it. Now seeing it before him, he must confront its lunacy. It occurs to him that he might, indeed, be out of his head. The wave of ecstasy he'd been surfing all day seems to have crested. He's lost his balance, and now he is flailing under the thunderous whitewater of its crash.

He paces around his living room and tries to reflect critically on the day. It had been totally out of synch with every other day of quarantine, anomalous even, in the broader scope of his life. He wasn't himself today. And he had no real reason to be; a faint and blurry flashback had triggered a full-on, like, manic episode?

There must be some kind of hidden Freudian message in the carnival. Or something happened that night that he's never fully processed. Maybe it had been filed in deep storage for a reason and something about the stressors of quarantine shook it loose. Like his subconscious is trying to tell him something.

Maybe this whole manic experience is just a biological response to late-stage quarantine. After so long without feeling any kind of love or intimacy, some survival mechanism in his brain just conjured up the opposite to soothe the lethal loneliness. Like hypothermia: after a point you begin to feel warm. As his limbic system atrophied from stress and lack of human contact, did it spasm and squeeze out a bunch of oxytocin just to see if it still could? And if such an intense feeling is only a chemical dump, just a push-button thing, then how real are any of his other emotions? Is there anything authentically "Kevin" about his feelings? Or are they just a spooky collection of chemicals and electricity, his consciousness merely the steam rising from a revved up meat machine?

Had he even stopped to really find out if that memory is in fact a memory at all? It could just as easily be completely confabulated, an inelegant Frankenstein of decaying memories clawing their way out of their shallow graves.

But it felt *so real.* He is shaking — if such an honest-to-God, felt-it-in-his-fucking-bones memory was wildly inaccurate, fraudulent even, what does that say about all his other memories?

The time has come to stalk Ally's Facebook in pursuit of hard evidence to corroborate his memories of her, proof that he is not losing his grip on his own past.

He navigates to her profile with a breathless anxiety and presses the left arrow, taking him to her very first uploads. He both recognizes her and doesn't, and with the photos come new memories that had previously evaded his search.

Winter formal freshman year, there he is. That definitely happened. He cringes upon seeing himself in that oversized suit, with his hair gelled with painfully self-conscious precision, his arm so awkwardly over Ally's shoulder. Then he remembers with a gasp that at the pre-dance photo-op party he'd had an anxiety-induced asthma attack and his mom had to run out to the car to get his inhaler and everything stopped and all the other moms freaked out and his friends watched from afar but Ally sat on the couch with him and rubbed his back and said nice things.

He clicks through more photos watching Ally mature in front of his eyes, glossing over a few group photos with the two of them in it. Then he gets to senior year and on the last day of school, when everyone wore their college t-shirts, the two of them stood beaming, arms over shoulders in the school courtyard.

He stops for a second to study this one.

Ally looks different than how he remembers her. He rehearses the memory of the carnival. He can at once hear her voice and see her face, and not. It dawns on him, rather horribly, that the woman at the carnival is not Ally. Well, it is. But it isn't. It is a cheap pastiche, a blurry outline of the girl he once knew, redrawn with too much poetic license. The woman at the carnival is an altogether new character, one of Kevin's own creation. And if this woman isn't really Ally, then who is he in love with?

He feels his chest tighten and he rises to find his inhaler. He grabs it off the table and takes two sharp puffs. The sun has long set, but he has yet to turn any lights on. He realizes this suddenly — that he is in the dark — but resists doing anything about it. Instead, he walks to the window and leans his forehead on the cold glass.

His sense of self falls from him like needles off a desiccated Christmas tree; all the things he thought he knew about himself lie in a heap at his feet. His conception of who he is, his understanding of the world at large, is based solely on memories of his lived experiences. But what has been altered, hidden, editorialized by his ego? And perhaps more troubling, what has been erased? He'd thoroughly repressed that memory of the asthma attack at formal. What other things has he done that he can't, or won't, remember? What if he's a monster and has no idea? What if he screamed at Ally at the carnival, left her stranded there, smacked her around later that night, or did something so unforgivable that it fried his circuit board and gave him amnesia just so he could keep living with himself?

Maybe he has no honest idea what kind of person he was in high school. What if his insistence on severing ties from Glenwood has been an effort to dodge any reminder of who he really is? Maybe Kevin, or maybe something separate from him — some autonomous biological mechanism, some cognitive CRISPR — has edited his memories into a tolerable life story, a final cut watchable enough to keep him from storming out of the theater.

What aspects of himself can be known with any objective certainty? Knowledge of who he is will forever be too warped by his own vision of himself, his own self-constructed narrative, that perhaps he can never truly know who he was back then, or by extension, who he is now. If he was able to misremember

Ally to the point of creating a new character, who's to say he hasn't done the same for himself? As he gets older and memories become more distant, they become more like dreams than anything. The tail end of his being unravels as it slithers on through time, like a fraying rope that can only be so long. Perhaps his actual self only exists for a handful of years — days, hours, even? — everything beyond that is slowly denaturing back into raw undefined existence.

He feels untethered, adrift. He is deeply frightened, as if waking up the morning after a drunken blackout in a bed that isn't his.

He hears his phone buzz on the couch. The screen fills his apartment with a blue glow. It vibrates in his hand as he studies the caller ID — a familiar area code.

"Hello?"

"Kevin? It's Ally. Ally Golden."

A rush of electricity runs up his neck and over his scalp.

"I got so excited when I saw your message. I figured I'd just call."

Her voice, just like her face, was different — realer — than he'd been able to conjure. It puts him at ease, like laughing gas at the dentist, and they catch up. She lives in Chicago and works for a marketing firm; it sounds like she enjoys it. She's engaged. Her fiancé sounds like a decent guy.

"So this is kind of random," he says, "But do you remember going to Glenwood Days with me? Right before leaving for college."

"Of course! I think that might have been the last time we hung out just the two of us."

"Did anything happen that night? That memory's just been on my mind lately and I don't know why."

"Not especially," she said. "I mean, we had a lot of fun. I remember that. You were so happy to finally be leaving Glenwood. We probably went on the Ferris wheel. And you know what? I think that was the night you showed me Explosions in the Sky. When you drove me home."

"You remember that?"

"Oh yeah. That was a big moment for me I think."

"Why's that?"

"Well, you really opened up to me. After five years you finally let me in."

"By showing you my secret playlist?"

She laughs gently. "No. That was the night you told me you'd started seeing a therapist. About the anxiety and panic attacks and how hard it had all been for you. And how college would be a fresh start. I feel like we talked for an hour in my driveway."

The memory leaps out at him like the hidden image in one of those optical illusion picture books. He remembers with a pang of shame how he failed to fight back tears when she asked him, warmly, "What's one thing you like about yourself?" The question echoes in his head, reverberating so loudly he can hardly hear Ally say:

"Now every time I hear Explosions in the Sky I think of you."

She announces that her fiancé has returned with dinner and that it was great to reconnect. She implores him to stay in touch.

"Keep being you, Kev," she says, and hangs up.

He drops the phone on his couch. Some specter in his mind has been vanquished, he feels lighter, emptier.

When he opens his laptop, he is greeted by the photo of him and Ally on the last day of school. This time he studies himself instead of her. It surprises him a little bit, like he might not recognize his high school self if he passed him on the street, like he is looking at a stranger who reminds him, only vaguely, of someone he has met before.

It dawns on him that the boy in that photo is indeed a stranger. There is no singular Kevin, but a million Kevins, not only existing in different points in time, but in the minds of everyone he's ever known.

He clicks to the right and he clicks again, glossing over a hundred different Ally Goldens until he sees the one he spoke to on the phone today. Then he goes to his own profile, opens his photos, and clicks left.

Slime Mold

I arrived in Eugene late in the afternoon. 4 o'clock maybe. It was hot. Pushing triple digits. The heat seemed to make the sun brighter. Harsher. The sky had a washed out quality to it, like faded denim. The only people outside were those with nowhere to hide. A deranged looking man in a tattered Thrasher shirt pushed a shopping cart full of scavenged refuse down the side-walk. He held up his pants with one hand and pushed the listing cart with the other. We locked eyes while I waited for the light to change.

Down the road was a sprawling encampment; dozens, maybe over a hundred tents clustered together in a park beneath a highway overpass. I imagined the people languishing under those tents, breathing heavily in the heat, the ground damp and pulverized like at a music festival. There was a row of five port-a-johns, the doors spray painted, one word each, to read ALL THIS COULD BE YOURS.

I was not especially distressed by this. My observations were cold and indifferent, made from behind sunglasses. I'm from Oakland, after all; it's part of the landscape. A lot of my friends and classmates lost their homes in 2008. I almost did, too. There was a night my mom made arrangements for us to move in with her brother in Concord. We even started packing. It never came to that, though.

I still lived with my mom. Or I did. I'd moved out that morning. Packed a few bags, threw them in the back of the van and hit the road bright and early. It was time. It was well past time. Whatever love or pride I'd had for Oakland had boiled away leaving only a crusty resentment for the place. It was a two way street, though. That city hated me back. Oakland hated me first, actually. It wanted me gone, like a spiteful girlfriend who found it easier to make my life miserable than just out-and-out dump my ass. There was no space for me in that town, like I just didn't make the cut. I tried, though. I really did. I'd rented rooms with some friends, but inevitably my tips would dry up and I'd spend an entire month of income on a windowless basement apartment with some kind of slime mold growing in the corner. When the lockdowns closed the bar, I had no choice but to move back in with my mom, sleep in the twin bed I'd had since grade school, and get a gig-work job delivering Amazon packages in my mom's old minivan. At some point it became about principle, about dignity. Never again.

So when my buddy told me he knew a guy opening a brewery in Eugene in need of a bartender, I said put me in, coach. "I'm all in, baby!" I said. "I'm moving to Eugene bay-bee!" And even before I got on the line with the manager, I was watching YouTube videos about my new home, imagining a new life up north, away from the Jeff Bezos wannabes and Elon Musk acolytes, in a small city with space to spare, where I could finally plant my flag. I had enough money saved up to put a downpayment on a new apartment and get situated before the brewery's opening night.

Turns out I was a little naive.

I'd rented an Airbnb for a week, assuming that was all the time I would need to find a place to live. It was a room in a mansion in the hills south of the city. Pricey, but the only one available at such short notice.

"What brings you to town?" my host asked. Her name was Margot. If I had to guess, I'd say she taught a high-end yoga class, or like, had a bespoke essential oil business.

"I'm moving here."

"Eugene is such a lovely place. You'll love it here. Too many homeless people, but you can avoid them."

I followed her down the stairs.

"What part of town will you be living in?"

"I don't have a place yet."

"Good luck," she said, but not in a cheerful way. "Housing is tight around here. Louie and I own a few rentals and they get snapped up almost immediately. The last one we got 36 applications on the first day."

"How'd you decide?"

"On what?"

"Who got the rental."

"We ended up renting to a friend. And this —" she said, "is your room."

It was nice. Just enough space to walk around the queen sized bed that filled the room. Large windows looked out on an expansive garden — at least an acre or two — with its own little trail system and koi pond.

"Feel free to explore the garden," she said. "There's all sorts of places to sit. Louie and I love having different places to sit."

She showed me to the bathroom and the back porch.

"We have another guest here as well. Braydon — I think that's his name — is in the suite down the hall. I'm sure you'll run into him."

Margot went back inside and I quickly pulled out my phone. I'd just assumed that nowhere was as unlivable as the Bay Area. I mean, how could a town like Eugene be that crowded? Zillow had some listings. Craigslist had a few ads. But all out of my price range. Anything even remotely affordable seemed to be chock full. There weren't even any ads seeking roommates or sublets. I wasn't about to let it spook me, though. I was in Eugene, baby! It was 2021! My fresh start begins tomorrow, I told myself.

I scheduled a handful of viewings while lying in bed. They were all apartment complexes with names like "Riverbank Court," "Evergreen Valley" and "Creekside Terrace." The faux-chic names somehow augmented their dreariness, like the names were the sole cynical attempt to pretend the complex was a place people wanted to live. None of them looked especially nice even on the website. They bordered highways or strip malls and their Google reviews were almost laughably hateful. And that was all fine by me. It was what I could afford, really. I was under no delusion of my net worth, and all I wanted was my own space — it did not have to be luxurious.

Riverbank Court was my first stop. The pool, so prominently advertised on the website, was green and fetid. A woman my age welcomed me into the leasing office.

"I'm here for the tour," I said.

She looked surprised.

"Of an apartment?"

"I registered on your website this morning."

"Oh," she said. "Yeah. So we actually don't have anything available for rent."

"Really? You posted six separate ads on Craigslist this morning. And every day last week."

"Yeah, sorry. We are taking applications for our waitlist, though."

"But then why did all the ads on Craigslist say you had move-in ready rooms?"

"I don't know anything about that. That comes from Seattle."

"Seattle?"

"That's where our headquarters are. I'm sorry, man. I don't have any answers for you. I just work for the property management company. All I can tell you is we don't have anything for rent."

Defeated, I asked: "How long is the waitlist?"

She opened a filing cabinet and walked her fingers along a line of dog-eared folder tabs.

"Looks like 26."

"So if I were to go on the waitlist, 26 other people would have to pass on the room before you called me?"

"Pretty much."

"How do I get on the waitlist?"

"Fill out an application and pay the 50 dollar fee."

"50 dollars? And pretty much a zero percent chance that I get the room?"

"Yup," she said, tiring of the interaction.

I sighed and looked up at the ceiling fan for a minute. It teetered on its axis and made no appreciable breeze. "Do you know if there are any other apartments around town that have availabilities?"

"When are you looking to move in?"

"As soon as possible."

"For sure not. I check in with other property managers every week. There are no vacancies anywhere."

"So the other apartments I signed up to tour today are also lying about having rooms?"

"Evergreen and Creekside?"

"How'd you know?"

"We own those, too. And they for sure don't have any vacancies."

"How many apartment complexes do you own?"

"I don't own any," she said, maybe waiting for a laugh, "but the management company has 17 in Seattle, I think 20 in Portland, and five in Eugene. They just bought one in Bend as well."

The conversation had run its course, and the property manager was looking around her desk for something to do. But I couldn't let go. I don't know if it was sympathy or answers I was waiting for, or if I was just biding time before facing reality.

"What do I do? I need a place to live."

"I don't know what to tell you. It's hard out here. I guess your best bet is to get on as many waitlists as possible. Get an Airbnb? Convert a van? I don't know."

I looked back up at the ceiling fan before audibly sighing and asking for a waitlist application. I filled it out, paid her, and as

I walked out she wished me good luck with a touch of sincerity and perhaps a pang of guilt.

I went back to my van and sat behind the wheel with the engine off and windows up. There was something bracing about the stale heat. I twisted around and studied the pulverized carpeting, the narrow metal tracks where the seats used to be, and the sum total of my earthly possessions piled on top. I wondered blankly how much stuff I'd have to throw out to sleep back there.

I heard the same thing at every leasing office. Even places with big "leasing now" signs out front told me sleepily that there was no room at the inn. For a small fee, though, I could get on the waitlist. Non-refundable, of course. The grift was becoming clear, and after dropping another 50 dollars to get on the waitlist at a truly dismal complex across from the I-5 interchange, hopelessness began to roll in like a thick ocean fog. How could so many people be chomping at the bit to live in such a shitty place? Where are all the other people on those waitlists now? Like, where do they wait? And who are they? Hard-up families, divorcés, single moms, widows, migrants, down-and-outs on the rebound, all with the one simple desire to have a place to call their own. Just a few hundred square feet where they can feel like they inhabit this world rather than just take up space in it.

I scoped out another dozen places in Springfield, too. It was as bleak as expected. The afternoon heat was peaking, and the air had a yellowish dirty-window flavor courtesy of the nearby wildfires. At Courtyard Estates, even the trees looked sad, their leaves wilted. A jowly man waiting for his aging dog to shit on the dead grass outside the leasing office really nailed the vibe.

Inside, a slovenly man sat limply behind a computer, playing Solitaire by the looks of it. Minesweeper maybe.

"Excuse me," I announced. "Do you have any apartments available to rent?"

He looked up like he hadn't heard me come in.

"Depends on who's asking."

His shirt had sweat stains, his tie was loose. He hadn't shaved in a few days. He held eye contact for a second before smiling broadly and rising from his chair. He stuck out his hand. "I'm just kidding. I'm Jim. I'd be happy to show you around."

He picked the keys up off his desk and we walked across the parking lot to the model room.

"So here's the deal," he said. "We might have a room available."

"You might?"

"We're in the process of evicting the tenant. The eviction moratorium expired last week so they're getting the heave-ho."

"Damn."

"Yeah, it's a lady and her kid. Tough, right? She's got long Covid or something and can't work any more."

"You're just going to put them out on the street?"

"Hey, whoa," he said, putting his hands up. "If it was up to me I'd let them stay."

He finally added: "I'm sure they'll land on their feet."

The apartment itself was not inspiring. The carpet was yellowing with age and a yappy little dog was going off on the other side of a paper-thin wall.

"Unfortunately there's no air conditioning in any of the units," he said.

I poked around the corners and inspected the kitchen. A menacing patch of mold grew tumor-like under the sink.

"When will you know if the apartment is available?"

"They're in court right now actually. We should know by the end of the day."

The heat was getting to me, and the closeness of the apartment added to my incipient nausea.

Back in the leasing office I filled out an application and shelled out yet another 50 bucks.

"I'll give you a call when I know about the availability."

"Do you have any other leads?" I asked. "In case this doesn't work out."

"You know," he said. "I don't know how wide of a net you're casting, but I heard there's an open house in Cottage Grove at 5:30 tonight. One bedroom duplex, I think. As far as I know they're only taking applications at the open house, so you'll want to be the first one there. To improve your chances."

I thanked him for his time and went back out into the sun. I kind of hoped to never hear from him again.

After Courtyard Estates I gave up for the afternoon. I returned to the Airbnb thinking I'd have the place to myself, enjoy the peace and quiet. I found, though, Margot listening to Bruno Mars on some house-wide sound system, drinking wine, and talking uproariously on the phone. My room was no refuge from any of that, so I went out to the back porch hoping to lay out on the couch with a complementary LaCroix from the guest fridge. Alas: The last LaCroix was gone and there was a man sitting on the couch, drinking the coveted beverage.

"Mind if I join you," I asked as I went to sit on a swing chair hanging from the rafters.

He introduced himself as Braydon, staying at the end of the hall. He was well into his forties and had thinning hair that he no doubt agonized over. He was portly, too, and had a beard that he probably thought looked good but was undeniably pubic. His clothes, though, were what really drew the eye. Dark skinny jeans, a white t-shirt and some kind of vinyl bomber jacket. It was like one of those American Flag outfits where it looks like the whole thing is made of a single repurposed flag. Instead of the flag, though, this jacket — sleeves and all — was the canvas of some chaotic surrealist painting. Dozens and dozens of deathly pale white people, all naked and, like, eating fruit and frolicking in the grass.

"Sweet jacket," I said, more curious than anything.

"Oh, thanks." He looked down at it nonchalantly. "It's Heironymous Bosch."

"Is that a designer?"

He scoffed. "Try early renaissance Dutch painter. I saw the original triptych in the Museo Del Prado in Madrid. When I saw this jacket in the gift shop I just had to have it."

I allowed for a few seconds of silence before I started to rise from the swing chair to make an exit.

"How long are you staying?" he asked.

"Hopefully only a week. I'm looking for a place."

"You and me both," he said. "I just closed on a property today."

"Congratulations," I said dryly. "Where are you moving from?"

"LA," he said, looking at his phone. "I'm not really moving. I just wanted a little place in the woods. A little getaway from the city."

I should have known. His speech, his posture, how he sipped that LaCroix — it all reeked of that self-obsessed aloofness found only in Los Angeles.

The glass door slid open with a heavy swoosh and out stepped Margot and Louie, each with a glass of red wine in hand.

"Good evening," she declared grandly, decidedly drunk. "Louie, this is Miles, our new Airbnb guest. And you've already met Braydon."

Louie was short, 5'4" at best, and bald. Shiny bald. He had a gold earring and a snow-white soul patch. "Hope you're enjoying your stay so far," he said. His voice was high, munchkin-like, and he, too, was well into the sauce. He'd already spilled a drop on his flowy linen shirt.

"Margot tells me congratulations are in order," he said to Braydon.

"Indeed," he said, finally putting away his phone. "I managed to get them down under a million."

"Good show! And how many acres?"

"Ten."

"Brilliant."

"And the best part is I can clear cut the entire lot and sell the lumber for essentially as much as the listing price. It pays for itself."

"We did the same thing when we built our mountain home in Bend. Congratulations. And what area of town?"

"South. Off Loraine Highway."

"Ah. Beautiful area. Beautiful. And no homeless people that far south."

"Ugh, I know. I thought of that. How do you stand it?"

"It's terrible. Getting worse. We don't get many out this way, but going into town is a nightmare. They're everywhere. Just milling about and talking to themselves and getting in the way."

"It's disgusting," Margot said. "Absolutely vile. They're always drunk or on drugs. Springfield has the right idea. Get thrown in jail for panhandling. And get fined 500 dollars for giving money to a homeless person. That's how it's done! No homeless people in Springfield."

"Miles," Louie said to me, "I hear you're also looking for a place."

I nodded.

"Renting?"

"That's the plan."

"The rental market is tough. Prices are going way up. All of our tenants are staying put. We've got a few houses around town and everyone is staying put. We're even thinking of renting out our house on the coast because demand is so high. Where are you looking?"

"Everywhere. I'm actually about to go to an open house in Cottage Grove."

"Cottage Grove is delightful. We've been thinking of snapping up a little property around there. Maybe starting a weed farm. Wouldn't that be fun, Margot? The little downtown area is so quaint."

"I really better get going."

The blood thumping in my ears wasn't loud enough to drown out the self-impressed chatter coming from the back porch. Even from the road I could hear them, their Hapsburgian narcissism breaching the boundary of their fatuous lives. Even in my car, the door closed, my jaw clamped shut, I could still hear them chortling and guffawing, enjoying their plush box seats while the rest of us fight to the death in the sand below.

It took about half an hour to get to Cottage Grove. I had a headache from the heat and the fatigue and the furious gnashing of teeth. It was a far cry from Eugene, just a small country town with a main street and older looking houses. Hardly what I'd had in mind for my new independent adventure, but I'd take it. I'd live in a storage unit if I could call it my own.

The 1-bedroom in question was a part of a duplex not far off the main street. I drove slowly looking for the house number, but my heart sank when, ahead of me, I saw a cluster of cars and a gaggle of antsy people on the sidewalk. I parked on the curb behind an old SUV piled high like some kind of Dust Bowl Okie mobile, the rear window blocked by a tetris of tarps and clothes and stuffed garbage bags.

The open house started at 5:30, and with five minutes to spare, dozens of prospective tenants were crowding the waist-high yard fence like it was a Best Buy on Black Friday. There were young couples, families with little kids, retirees, immigrants, sad single people of all ages.

"Is that you?" one of them asked me, nodding towards my van. He wore a flat brim Monster Energy hat and bounced a baby in his arm.

"Yeah, that's me."

He scoffed and shook his head. As he turned away he said: "Another fucking Californian. Unbelievable."

The woman with him, presumably his partner, glared at me with powerful contempt.

"Hey. Whoa. I deserve a place to live too," I said, in no mood to be pushed around.

The guy whipped back around and lunged toward me. "No you don't. You absolutely fucking don't. You California people come up here with your money thinking you can have whatever you want. Like all this is here just for you. And you push the rest of us out to make space for yourself and your bullshit. This is my home. I deserve to live here. Not you. My family has been here for generations and now we've got nowhere to go. You're not entitled to just live wherever you want. Fucking go home."

I stared him down, the two of us debating whether to escalate this. I was ready to. Were it not for the baby in his arms I might have gotten right up in his face and tipped that stupid hat right off his head. Instead I went with this:

"Funny. I bet some Indian said the same thing to your shithead grandpappy when he rolled up here."

He handed the baby off to his partner.

"What did you say to me?"

"I said you should fucking get over yourself."

He took a step towards me and I was ready to rip into this man. I was enraged in a primal way, like a pissed off bear ready to risk it all for my territory, for my claim to the world. Just then, though, the real estate agent appeared on the front stoop like Willy Wonka and strolled down the yard to open up the gate. The crowd funneled in hastily, and my would-be challenger turned to push his way to the front.

I hung back on the sidewalk. My rage gave way to an empty sadness as I watched the houseless masses squeeze their way through the garden gate like spooked sheep through a corral. I turned to leave, but caught myself staring at the slovenly SUV parked in front of me, wondering absently if maybe it belonged to the Monster Energy guy.

My phone rang as I dug in my pocket for my keys.

"Miles? This is Jim from Courtyard Estates. Today's your lucky day."

The eviction had been upheld.

"Here's the thing: Because you don't have proof of income, you're going to have to put down first and last month's rent at the signing, as well as a security deposit equal to one month's rent."

Damn near every dollar I had.

"If you don't have the cash by tomorrow, I'll have to offer it to someone else."

"No," I said. "I'll do it. I've got the cash."

"Perfect. I'll see you tomorrow at 9AM to sign the lease."

On the drive back to Eugene I thought about my new apartment, not with relief or excitement, but dread. I saw myself sitting in a fold-up camp chair in the middle of my empty, yellowing living room, listening to the neighbor's yapping dog, the upstairs tenant's rap music, the rattle and buzz of the moribund refrigerator, the interminable drip of the leaky faucets. I saw the slime mold metastasizing in the dark and humid corners, its tendrils extending blindly into every chanced upon crevice, smothering every obstacle, consuming every morsel of decay and detritus, not out of malice or selfishness but some primordial drive to expand.

I turned on the radio. NPR. The lead story was that Jeff Bezos had just returned from his first joyride to space. It cut to the post-touchdown press conference. Bezos was giddy.

"I also want to thank every Amazon employee and every Amazon customer," he said. "You paid for this."

Death Metal

My name is Dennis. I'm from Alabama and I like metal. I like listening to it real loud in my room and in my car. I like going to shows that are real loud and have crazy mosh pits. My favorite kinds of metal are death metal and powerviolence. I also like grindcore. Sometimes I put on my headphones and totally spaz out when nobody's looking. Like I'm out there headbanging and swinging my fists and roundhouse kicking, but I'm just in my room by myself and the rest of the world is quiet except for in my head.

I have the most metal job in the world. My job is so metal. Every time I tell people about my job they're like "Wow, that's so metal," or "That's hardcore, bro." So now I get more cred in the metal scene because my job is so freaking metal.

I work for the City of Tucson. Actually I work for Pima County. I work in the Office of Medical Examination which means I scoop up geezers for a living. When someone dies in Pima County, they sometimes need someone to move the body. Maybe the paramedics are busy, or maybe the person is just super dead and they don't need an ambulance. Or sometimes it's just too gross and the paramedics don't want to do it. Then they call my office and my office sends me out there to scoop up that geezer.

People always want to know how I got my job because it's so metal. They all must think I'm a total wizard, like I'm a total metalhead or something to get a job this metal. And that's probably true. I'm pretty metal. See, I'm from Alabama and I came out to Tucson because Tucson has the gnarliest metal scene in the country. Every hardcore metal band has to play a show in Tucson if they want any cred. So after I got my grandma's car, after she croaked, I just drove all the way out here. I didn't know anyone, so at first I just lived in my grandma's car for a few days. But I went to a few shows and met some real good people. For some reason they all asked me if I was from Greenbow, Alabama. But I'd never heard of no place called Greenbow. So I always said no, I'm from Phenix City, Alabama, and they seemed to think that was funny somehow. And then they'd ask me if I ran all the way here from Alabama, and I always said no, that would be crazy. But maybe they figured I was in good shape, because I am pretty thin and wiry looking. And sometimes they'd ask me if I knew their friend Jenny, and I said I knew a Jenny but she probably wasn't their friend. They all thought that I was real funny. Which was fun, because people never thought of me as funny before. But there was one guy named Emmet who would tell them all to go fuck themselves or, like, eat shit or whatever anytime they started asking me about Greenbow or saying "run, Dennis, run" anytime I went to the bathroom or to get beers.

Emmet's a real good guy. Maybe the best guy I know. He invited me into the group chat so I could meet up with him and his friends at different shows. He's big. Not fat, just big. And he's got a square jaw. But he's kind of moody, I guess. I don't know if I've ever seen him really laugh at something. And he's got this sort of curly black hair that hangs over his eyes most of the time. He doesn't look like he'd be a nice guy, but he really is. One night, we were at Mr. Head's on 4th Ave after a show, which is where all the punks and metalheads like to hang out when the shows are all over. When I told him I was staying in my car, he even told me to come stay at his house and crash in his guest room. He had a nice house in Midtown. He said his mom died a year ago and now it was all his. He also said I had to get a job and pay rent because "the mortgage won't pay itself."

The only thing was that he had a cat. I'm not allergic or anything, but he made a big deal about it. 90% of his house rules had to do with being nice to Penny. She was super old. He told me not to touch her because she was too old. She kept to herself and she spent most of her time on the couch wrapped in a fuzzy pink blanket with little Hello Kitty faces on it. We never sat on the couch. Emmet got us fold-out camp chairs for watching tv.

She was pretty, though. She was all gray, all the same dusty color gray. She had a pink collar and eyes like jewels. Gosh, Emmet really loved that cat. He fed her fancy cat food and filled her bowl with water from the Britta jug. And he would lightly headbutt her to say hello and goodbye. He would massage her face sometimes. But mostly he just left her alone. Sometimes the best gift you can give someone is space, he would say.

Emmet even helped me get a job. That same weekend I moved in he showed me how to make a resume. And it's a pretty metal resume. My last job back in Alabama was at a slaughterhouse. You know, where all the pigs get killed. And gosh, you wouldn't believe how many pigs got killed every day. I guess they're still out there killing pigs right now. There was an endless line of pigs coming down the conveyor belt. A big ole truck would back up to the loading bay and the pigs would run out single file into this chute that was also a conveyor belt, and at the end a big ole clamp came down around the pig's neck — kind of like those ones in medieval town squares — and held it still while an air compressor shot a hole clear through its head. Darla got to work the air compressor. She was old and fat and only had one arm, and because she'd worked there for so long, she got to be the one to push the button. She let me push it once. What a sound! Pfft, splat. And then the pig just went real still. Because it was in the clamp, it didn't fall over or anything. Right after that, another clamp shuts on its back legs and lifts it up way off the ground so that it hangs upside down. Then it starts moving like a dress shirt at a dry cleaners until a buzz saw cuts its throat and they leave it to hang so that all the blood drips out of it. That takes a little time. But after that, it moves on to another buzz saw that slices right down the middle and all the guts fall out. Another crazy sound! What's even crazier is that the ground under the pig slopes down, so you can see all the guts slide into some mystery pit under the floor. The guts make this sort of sucking sound as they slide down. But you have to listen really hard to hear it because it's super loud in the slaughterhouse. It's like being at a metal show. All the buzz saws and machinery and all the pigs squealing all came together to make like a real hardcore metal band. The saws were like the guitars and the lurching conveyor belt was like the drums and the squealing pigs were like the cymbals. And I was the singer because I got to use the hose. After the pig got split open it came to my station where I used a pressure hose to blast out all the blood clots. The hose made this low grumble when I turned it on, and then when I pulled the trigger it made this whooshing roar and when it hit the pig it sounded sort of like rain on a tent but super loud. All the leftover blood and gunk comes flying out all over the place like when you wash a spoon too close to the faucet. It's crazy. Like a 10 hour metal show every day.

Emmet told me that I didn't have space for all that in my resume, though.

The next day he took me to work with him and introduced me to his boss. Emmet also works for the Office of Medical Examination. He also scoops geezers for a living. He was working the afternoon shift, but we got there a half hour early so that I could talk to his boss.

The office was pretty spooky. It was in the basement of this building by the hospital. The hallways were really wide and the floor was this white tile that made me think of a highway rest stop bathroom. It smelled kind of that way too. Like those urinal cakes. The boss' office was way at the end of this hallway and it was dark like a closet and lit with one of those light bulbs in the ceiling that has a chain coming down from it to turn it on and off. There was a desk with a computer and stacks and folders wrapped with rubber bands.

"Who is this?" He asked. He was super fat — like with fat rolls and everything — and he had a five o'clock shadow. He didn't seem very friendly. He looked like the kind of guy who smoked cigars and farted really loud but would glare at you if you laughed.

"This is Dennis."

The boss looked at me like I'd just barfed on him.

"My name is Dennis. I'm from Alabama."

"Jesus Christ," he said. "What the fuck, Emmet?"

"He's a good guy. He's not squeamish."

He stared down Emmet for a second and then looked over at me. He held out his hand and snapped his fingers. Emmet elbowed me and nodded at the folder I was carrying. I'd brought my resume in a folder because it looked more professional.

"Come on already," he said.

He read my resume and asked me some questions.

"You worked at a Denny's?"

"Yes sir. I washed the dishes there when I was in high school."

"Did you finish?"

"Yes sir, I finished washing the dishes every night."

"No, high school. Did you finish high school?"

"Yes sir, I finished going to high school."

"What year did you graduate?"

"Oh, I didn't graduate. I just finished going to high school."

He looked at me funny for a second.

"And you worked at a slaughterhouse?"

"Yes sir. I did that for three years after I finished high school."

"What was that like?"

"It was really metal, sir."

He looked at Emmet. "What does that mean?"

"It was just really metal, sir."

"I heard you. But what do you mean when you say something is metal?"

I didn't really know how to describe it. "You know the sound when a fork gets stuck in a garbage disposal?"

"Sure."

"It's like that sound, but if it was a feeling."

He looked back at Emmet. "What the fuck is he talking about?"

"He's captivated by the primal power of it all. Awed by the raw brutality. Metal is kind of a religion for him," Emmet said. "There's an honesty to it."

The boss rolled his eyes and went back to looking at my resume.

"It says here that you 'pressure washed the carcasses'?"

"Yes sir."

"Was there a lot of blood?"

"Yes sir. They gave me a special white uniform with a hood and goggles on account of all the blood."

"Did that bother you?"

"No sir. But it did bother me when the fellas said I looked like a used tampon."

"It also says you were 'responsible for the heads'?"

"Yes sir. At the end of the day my job was to toss the heads into the compactor. And then I'd turn on the compactor and make sure all the heads got crushed up enough to be tossed in the trash or fed to cows or something."

"That's pretty metal all right."

"Be cool, Ed," Emmet said. I'm not sure why, though. The head crusher was super metal.

The boss was sort of smiling now. I think maybe I was impressing him. The head crusher is usually pretty impressive.

"Why did you leave that job if it was so metal?"

"Well, sir, my grandma died and the bank took her trailer so I had nowhere to live. And I always figured the desert was the most metal place on earth with all the scorpions and black widows. And everything has thorns."

"I'll give you that," he said. "All right," he said. "Thanks for coming by."

I started to get up.

"Ed…" Emmet said.

"Get real, Emmet. I can't hire this guy."

"Fuck off, Ed. I'm sick of this short-staffed bullshit. I'm out here hoisting geezers on my own. You either hire Dennis to be my partner or I'm walking."

The boss leaned back in his chair. It was one of those swivel chairs and it creaked so loud I thought it was going to snap. He glared at Emmet real hard like he was thinking about choking him out. After a while he looked back at me.

"Fine," he said. "Ok," he said. "You think you can handle this?" He was looking at me now. "You know what this job is?"

"Yes sir. I can do it."

"Oh yeah?" He stared me down for a second. "Have you ever seen a dead body? A dead human body?"

"Yes sir, I have."

"Really now? Tell me about it."

"Well, one day I came home from school and my mama was dead on the couch."

I waited for him to say something, but he didn't.

"I went to shake her awake but a bunch of barf fell out of her mouth and all over her shirt. I thought maybe she'd just drank too much again so I left her alone. But she was still there when I went to school the next morning. I figured she was definitely dead because the flies were all over her and coming out of her mouth. My grandma said she took too many of her back pain pills."

The boss didn't look mean or confused anymore. He wasn't even looking at me.

"You'll be perfect," he said.

He put my resume in the drawer behind his desk and slammed it shut. He kind of grumbled the rest.

"I'll send it up to HR. Come in tomorrow at 9 for your training."

"Did I get the job?" I looked up at Emmet. He nodded. I thought the boss'd pull out some cigars and slap me on the back, but everyone just seemed a little sad.

For training all I had to do was watch a movie. The boss rolled in a tv like they would do in high school, except we were in one of those white-tiled rest stop-smelling rooms. He didn't say anything when I said good morning, and he didn't tell me about his weekend when I asked. All he said was I had to watch the video and then I was Emmet's problem.

On the video a Mexican fella and a lady with big hair talked about how to lift with your knees and not with your back. And to wear gloves like doctors wear. And to always "survey the scene" for potential dangers. Then there was a whole thing about watching out for needles because you don't want to get poked. You also got to be careful to not get any blood or poop on you, or at least as little as possible. Apparently that's a thing – watching out for poop. Emmet told me later when I asked that the last thing you do before you die is "cake your shorts." Emmet said that everyone's last act on this Earth is to take one last big runny shit before giving up the ghost. Like, everyone. It's one thing we all have in common. Even the pigs at the slaughter-house; they'd spray the pig behind 'em with a big blast of shit the second the air hose went through their heads. But they don't show that in movies. When people die it's all dramatic and poetic. But it turns out everyone's last words are followed by a wet nasty shart.

After watching the video, Emmet showed me the morgue. It was so freaking metal. The freezer closets that the bodies go in clang shut like a prison cell. And they got all kinds of crazy knives and hoses and little saws that look like dentist tools in there to poke around in the corpses. He introduced me to the medical examiner, but all she did was nod at me. Then Emmet showed me the locker room and gave me my new uniform. It was a gray short sleeve button up and it said OME in big letters on the back. It came with these gray pants too. Emmet said I could go buy some non-slip shoes at the Pay Less after work.

I learned a ton of stuff my first few weeks on the job with Emmet. For starters, you're never supposed to grab a decomp by the arms because you could "de-glove" them. Emmet warned me, but I didn't listen and had to learn the hard way.

I also learned that the desert can eat an entire body down to the bone in three days. So freaking metal. We picked up a lady who croaked in her backyard, and by the time we got there she already had like a beard of maggots crawling on her face and something had already eaten her eyes out of her head and so the maggots were wriggling around in her eyeholes too.

I also learned what happens if you die in a hot tub. This one fat geezer croaked in his jacuzzi but no one found him for like three days. And apparently the hot water and jets had been on the whole time, so when Emmet and I got there it was like fat-guy soup. It was like one of those cartoon witch's cauldrons with bones floating on top and big bubbles suddenly burping up out of nowhere. We had to scoop him out in buckets. Well, I had to scoop him out because Emmet started barfing and couldn't handle it. He had to wait out by the van. When I carried out the last two buckets, I saw Emmet's face was all wet like he'd been crying but he said that it was just from throwing up so hard.

I also learned that some people really lose their goddamn minds over dead bodies. Like, this one time Emmet and I had to go scoop up an old abuela, but her whole family was still in the house. I mean *the whole* family. There was probably fifteen of them - kids, parents, aunties, uncles, more abuelas. And holy cow, they were really going at it. Howling and moaning and crying. One of the aunties was on her knees on the floor by the couch gripping the dead abuela's blouse and wouldn't let her go even as Emmet and I were trying to scoop her. And then they started tugging on us, too. Emmet was trying to say things in Spanish but no one was listening.

When we finally got her in the bag and were wheeling her out to the van that same auntie tried yanking the abuela back off the gurney and pushed me out of the way trying to unzip the bag. One of the uncles had to hold her back. She finally fell down and sat on the concrete and I swear the whole freaking world fell out of her.

Emmet let me drive that one to the morgue.

Oh, and cockroaches. They can eat literally anything. One time, we got called to this dope hole in Flowing Wells to pick up some ODs. We met another crew there on account of there being too many bodies for one van. They were already in there, Armando and Phillip I think were their names. And boy, they were having a good time. Laughing hysterically looking at Armando's phone.

"Look at this," he said, and called me over.

He'd taken a picture of one of the dead tweekers. He was skinny and kind of purple-looking and the needle was still sticking out of his arm. His head was craned back over this ratty, ripped up couch and his mouth was wide open. He was covered in cockroaches. Head to toe. They weren't crawling, though. They were latched on like moths on a screen door, because I guess that's how they eat.

"How about: What's eating you?" Armando said, and they started cracking up even harder.

"Wait, wait" Phillip said. He had to catch his breath. "What about: Papa Roach reunion tour!"

They were doubled over laughing, so I figured I ought to start laughing, too.

"This is it," Armando said. "This is my dankest meme yet."

I looked over and saw Emmet standing in the room with all the dead tweekers. There were four of them slumped over in different parts of the room. Two of them were spooning on a rotten mattress. Emmet had the folded up bags in his hand, but he wasn't laying them out. He was just staring, and he just stood there while I took the bags out of his hand. He wouldn't even help me scrape the roaches off.

"Come on, Emmet," I said. But he was frozen. Apparently they went to high school together or something. Emmet and the tweekers. Or he grew up with one of them? I forget. He told me to shut the fuck up with the cockroach facts on the drive back to the morgue.

The other day we were kicking it in the van. We'd just scooped a super metal car accident. A real "peel job." It was lunchtime and I wanted a chicken sandwich, so we went to Raisin' Canes. Emmet said he wasn't hungry. I said I didn't believe him. I hadn't seen him eat in days, and how could someone not want a chicken sandwich?

So I asked him: "What's eating you?"

He kept looking out the window, but he said, "I'm worried about Penny."

"Because she's about to die?" I asked.

He didn't say anything.

"Why don't you just put her down?" I'd actually been wondering about this for a while. "I think the vet will do it if you don't want to do it yourself."

He still didn't say anything, and I wasn't sure if he'd heard me.

"Or I could do it if you don't want to pay for it."

Then he whipped around real angrily.

"Don't you ever touch Penny," he said. "Don't you ever fucking go near her."

I stopped chewing my chicken sandwich and we just looked at each other for a minute until his face got soft and he thumped his head against the headrest. He breathed out real heavy.

"I'm sorry," he said.

I went back to eating my chicken sandwich, but then he asked me:

"Dennis, what do you think dying feels like?"

I thought about it for a second while working on a big bite of chicken sandwich. "Well," I said, "I figure it's probably the most metal thing there is. Like, you know when you drive on the highway with the windows down? I'll bet it sounds like that, only times a million. And the car keeps going faster and faster, and the engine's working so hard it sounds like a monster mosquito in your head, and all the g-forces are pushing on you so hard you feel like you weigh a million pounds. And eventually you get going so fast that you just, like, break the speed of light and disappear."

"And then what?"

"And then it's just over."

"There's no afterlife?"

"Nah."

"So it's just blackness and silence?"

"Not even. Remember when we were watching *Planet Earth* the other night? And there was that super metal scene with the baby elephant that gets lost in the desert? And when it falls in the sand and finally gives up, the camera cuts away and suddenly that British guy is talking about flamingos or something?"

"Sure."

"I think it's like that. Like, the camera just cuts away. The universe just, like, stops paying attention to you."

Emmet didn't say anything back. He just kept looking right out the window.

"I mean, that elephant didn't go to no elephant heaven. Neither did all those pigs at the slaughterhouse. Doesn't that just sound silly to you? Like this chicken that I'm eating is bucking and pecking around heaven right now? If that were true, then cockroaches would also have to go to heaven after you squash them, and so would all the trees that get cut down to build houses, and that's just too silly. I just don't see why it would be any different for people."

Emmet turned on the van. "We should probably get going."

I asked him one more time if he was sure he didn't want a chicken sandwich, but he just pulled out onto the curb.

We usually got Wednesdays and Thursdays off. That was our weekend. I really wanted to go to a ghost town, you know, like in *Red Dead Redemption*. I was all ready to go bright and early, but Emmet was sitting on the couch with Penny. She was wrapped in her pink Hello Kitty blanket and Emmet held her and rocked her like she was a little baby. And boy did she look terrible. Her fur was all greasy and falling out in patches and you could see little scabs in the bald spots. And one of her eyes looked like it was about to fall out. Like, it wasn't the right color, and you could tell it was just sort of rolling around in there like a loose marble.

Emmet said he was going to stay home with Penny.

"But what about the ghost town?" I said.

He wouldn't take his eyes off Penny. She was shivering and would let out these little coughs and puffs that sounded like an empty can of whipped cream. He kept ignoring me; it was like I wasn't even there. So I just left without him.

I drove all the way out there and, boy, was I disappointed. It was a bunch of crumbling buildings and a few boring museum signs that said how the mine used to work. There were no ghost tours, or haunted mines, or spooky saloons. Not even a Ripley's Believe It Or Not. It was still kind of metal, though. I was the only one there, so I just ran around and made like I was in *Red Dead Redemption* and blasted metal on my iPhone.

When I got home I saw Emmet sitting out in the backyard. He was sitting in one of those camping chairs just staring at the dirt. I walked out there to tell him that the ghost town wasn't a real ghost town, but he didn't listen. I asked him if Penny finally croaked and he said yeah. He'd buried her right there, wrapped in her favorite pink blanket because he knew she would like that.

"You know why I like you so much, Dennis?" He was tracing circles in the dirt with a big ole twig. "You're the most honest man I've ever met."

I didn't really know what to say to that. I was busy thinking it was high time for me to finally sit on the couch now that Penny wasn't hogging it. I started backing away because Emmet was kind of weirding me out, but then he kept going:

"Like, you can't lie. You can't even lie to yourself. I'm out here lying to myself every day, trying to believe that I'm going to see my mom again, that I'll see Penny again. That all those geezers we scoop are finally in a better place, hanging out with all the people they'd spent their whole lives missing. But the minute Penny died I just couldn't keep deceiving myself anymore, no matter how bad I wanted to. All of a sudden, all that talk of God and heaven and spirits just deflated with a sputtering fart like an untied balloon. There was no ghost to give up. She just sort of made some noises and pissed and shit herself and went limp. There was nothing sacred or supernatural about it. Nothing spiritual. She was just meat. And I think you knew that all along."

He was quiet for a second. I tried to make a break for it, but then Emmet got even weirder.

"If there is anything supernatural about death, it's how goddamn permanent it is. There is some holy power — some real fucking heavy medicine — in how final it is. How infinite it is. How magnificently fucking silent it is. I think you get that, too. You're a holy man, Dennis. You're a freaking shaman, Dennis. You're Neo in the hallway at the end of *The Matrix*."

I said thanks, but then I said I needed to take a nap. Even as I was walking back into the house he kept saying, "You're a holy man, Dennis." I figured maybe he just needed some space.

He stayed out in the backyard for the rest of the day. He didn't come in until after dark. I snuck out to Popeye's for a chicken sandwich and ate it in the parking lot. Then I listened to metal and drove around thinking Emmet would be over Penny by the time I got back.

I don't think he was, though. He stayed in his room for the rest of the night.

The next morning I was frying myself some bacon for breakfast when I looked out the kitchen window and saw Penny's blanket stuck on some cacti in the backyard. I figured that wasn't right, so I went out to investigate and found little clumps of Penny's fur blowing in the dirt. Then I found one of her feet and then her head. Half of it still had fur on it, but on the other half her cheek had been ripped off so that you could see her teeth and her gums and the stringy muscles on her snout. It kind of looked like she was snarling at me. It was so metal. The hole where Emmet had stuck her was all dug up. Some of the local coyotes must of gotten a whiff of her in the night.

Emmet came out while I was poking at her head with a stick trying to get a good look at it. He was shouting "what the fuck, what the fuck" and he kept shouting it louder and louder and then he sort of walked around in little circles and pulled at his hair and squatted real low screaming "fuck it all!" But he was crying and his voice cracked and next thing you know he was sitting criss-cross apple sauce in the dirt sobbing and blubbering "fuck it all" over and over.

That's when I realized I'd forgotten about my bacon. I went back inside, but it was all burnt to ashes. Such a bummer. So I scraped it all into the trash and went to Chick-Fil-A for some chicken biscuits instead. I asked Emmet if I should get him one too, but I guess he wasn't hungry.

Dragons Projected

Lyle is unsure whether he has a test today in his Intermediate Computational Algorithms class. He's been unsure all day; in fact, he was wondering about it last night, but considered the effort to find the syllabus crumpled up in the bowels of his backpack not worth it. He thought about it while ripping bong this morning and decided that he could totally take the test high and kill it. Computer science is totally his thing. While playing StarCraft II with an hour to go before the possible test, he wondered if he should study just in case. And, what? Like, not play StarCraft II because of a possible test that he'll ace anyway?

On his walk to campus, an angsty pang grips his stomach. Should he have studied? Should he have not smoked that last bowl? Nah, it's fine, he tells himself. There probably isn't a test anyway. But like, what if all the drugs are finally starting to, like, fry his brain and he's just convinced himself that it's all good?

When he gets to class – one of those miniature lecture halls – he pulls out his gameboy and resumes training his Pokémon. He wonders if maybe he should pull out his textbook for a quick review before the might-be test. But what good would a few minutes do anyway? Plus, he's like minutes away from beating the Elite Four.

Someone slides a backpack off of a windbreaker, the nylon v. nylon contact gets Lyle's attention.

"Yo, Derek," he says, looking up from his gameboy.

"Yo."

"Do we have a test today?"

"No." He is confident at first, but then his eyeballs look up and to the right as he scans his memory. "I don't think so," he says with a hint of worry. Derek turns around to address the half-dozen computer science students sitting in the rows behind them.

"Do we have a test today?"

They all respond in the same way as Derek: incredulous at first, even slightly angry that he is introducing foggy concern into their otherwise sunshiny day. They all look at each other, a few dig into their backpacks to find a syllabus. The whole class is now involved, everyone whispering "there's definitely no test today, right?" to one and other. A responsible female with her syllabus at the front of her well-organized and sharpie-decorated Intermediate Computational Algorithms binder concludes decisively what everyone knew but didn't believe: no test. The class breathes a sigh of relief. Plus, their professor is now officially two minutes late; another indicator that there is no test. Unless he's late because he's printing 43 copies of an elaborate multi-paged exam.

"Yo, Lyle," Derek says.

"Yo," Lyle replies, deep in combat with a Gengar.

"Do you have any more of that acid? The Scooby-Doo tabs."

Lyle repeats the question slowly to himself, genuinely trying to retrieve the data from the sprung and overflowing file cabinets of his mind. He definitely does, but he's not sure how many tabs are left, and he wants to keep some for personal use.

"Yeah, I think so. I'll have to check."

Derek sucks his teeth and nods gently. His bottle cap glasses and bristly beard give him a classic early-1970's head/freak look. "Groovy."

The professor walks in all frazzled and apologizes for being late. Lyle yanks his attention from Derek only to see if he is carrying a stack of papers. Not today. Ha! And to think he almost wasted time preparing for a test. He returns to his Pokemon, but his brain snags like a knit sweater on a protruding nail. Why did he think he had a test in this class at all? Evidently there was no reason to. Is he confused with another class? Does he have a test in Intro to Data Mining? Maybe the test announcement he's thinking of is the neural echo of one that happened weeks ago. Temporally dislodged by all the drugs? Or did he dream of an impending test? If so, then why can't he remember that it was a dream? Is some sort of structure in his consciousness eroding? Dissolving? Rotting like a sweet tooth? Jesus Christ, has he finally done it? Has he erased the borders and labels of his mental map to the point where he can no longer differentiate between land and sea? Is Gengar moving? Is that a feature of the game? Or is he having some sort of acid flashback? Gengar's red eyes are subtly expanding and contracting, his menacing grin constantly growing, but not changing size.

"Do you have any more of that Scooby-Doo acid?"

"Yeah, I told you. I'll have to check."

Derek looks up from his notebook, one eyebrow raised. Lyle speaking at normal volume in the middle of a lecture makes him uncomfortable.

"Yeah. I heard you the first time," Derek whispers in a curt, shut-the-fuck-up tone.

Lyle's face gets all hot. His whole body feels like that moment when you pop a handful of Sour Patch Kids in your mouth and your glands squirt out so much saliva at once that it hurts. Did Derek not say anything? Holy shit, did he just hear a voice in his head? Or was it a memory that he confused as a real stimulus? Lyle is perspiring profusely. His eyes are darting around the room. If he gets up to leave, everyone will stare at him. Maybe they're all already staring at him. Is he making a scene? Oh fuck, why is it so quiet? Has the professor stopped class to stare at him too?

Wait a minute, wait a minute, wait a minute. He needs to calm down, take a deep breath, drink some water. The professor is advancing his PowerPoint. Everyone is taking notes. He concludes that he is not going crazy. If he was, he would be unable to question his sanity. Is that actually a real thing? Maybe that's just some bullshit they tell crazy people to get them to calm down. Fuck! No – he needs to shut up and think about this reasonably. He commences a full systems check.

Did he drop acid this morning and forget about it?

No chance, he concludes. He is able to account for all his actions this morning, although recalling specific memories – like how many games of StarCraft he played, which chair he sat in to eat breakfast – is not effortless; he must stretch as if diving for a fly ball just barely in reach. Regardless, he remembers everything, and with impressive detail. As long as all those memories are in fact real. Nope, ignore that, that's not helpful.

Did he accidentally touch a tab and absorb some acid that way?

Unlikely, but possible. All the Scooby-Doo tabs are locked up in his drug dealing safe, which he keeps hidden in the false bottom of his bookshelf. Could there have been an errant tab in his pocket? Or floating around in his backpack? Mental note(s): keep better track of all tabs of acid. And clean out backpack (wear gloves).

Is he having an acid flashback?

Entirely possible, although this one would be notably severe. Previous acid flashbacks merely inspired meandering strolls around the neighborhood and a profound love of ambient electronica. They are generally so mild, in fact, that Lyle could only label them as flashbacks in retrospect. Now the question is, why is this flashback so strong? Are strong flashbacks a characteristic of the Scooby-Doo acid? He'll have to ask his guy next time he buys from him. Or maybe it's because he had coffee this morning. Did he have coffee this morning? Yeah right after he... Oh wait. He totally *did* take acid this morning. Lyle lets out a snort of laughter. No wonder he's losing his mind, he's tripping balls. Slithering Jesus, that Scooby-Doo shit is strong.

Lyle pulls out his notebook and starts doodling pictures of Keebler elves smoking blunts and playing miniature golf. The lecture, he decides, is pretty interesting too. Now it's just a matter of deciding whether or not he has a test in his next class. Should he study now? Nah. He'll figure it out later.

Lyle makes it through the day without taking any tests, which is fortunate because he is only barely tethered to this world. Every time he lifts his foot off the ground, he gets this weird feeling that his leg is weightless, and that, were it not for some sort of loose magnetic attraction between him and the earth, he would float away like a helium balloon. But how strong are these magnets? If he were to start high-stepping, would the magnets in his feet break free from Earth's tractor beam? Maybe if he did it super slowly he could study the tensile strength of the magnets.

He tests his hypothesis while walking through the quad on his way to the dining hall, where the undergrad working the counter nervously asks for more personal space while Lyle pays for his meatball sub. At some point, a big gob of marinara sauce splats on his shirt, but he chooses not to wipe it off. If he wipes it off there will just be a red stain and people will know that he spilled on himself like an idiot, but if he leaves the chunky lump of sauce untouched maybe people will think it is intentional and like, trendy?

"Lyle!"

He looks up but doesn't see anybody. Spirit guides for his trip, perhaps?

"Lyle!"

He turns around and spies a familiar face.

"Erin!" She is small like a pixie and dressed hipster-chic, outfit replete with flannel shirt and big-framed glasses. A strand of her hair is dyed pink.

"I saw you, like, frog-marching in the quad?"

Her laugh can only be described as effervescent. For a second, Lyle thinks he might be in love with her.

"Are you busy tonight?" Erin asks.

"Define busy?"

"My boyfriend wants to buy some weed, thought maybe you could hook him up?"

"Since when do you have a boyfriend?"

"Since last weekend!"

"Unreal. That guy I saw you talking to at the bar on Saturday?"

"His name is Davis. He's super sweet."

Lyle screws up his face, earnestly trying to remember the guy. He places himself in the bar; it's crowded, he's drinking tequila, someone has just selected Fetty Wap on the jukebox. Is Fetty Wap's glass eye real? It's got to be a gimmick, right?

"What is a Trap Queen anyway?" he accidentally says out loud.

"What?"

"Hmm?"

Lyle finds himself enthralled with the perplexed but amused expression on Erin's face. He would describe her as "adorable" and he is instinctively suspicious of her assorted boyfriends, even though he was once one of them.

"Do you think you could get him some weed, though? It's for his roommates or something?"

"Sure. Yeah. Totally."

"His house is throwing a party tonight. 469 Crosby. Could you swing by?"

He nods energetically.

"Great! And you've got something on your shirt?"

Lyle looks down at the gob of marinara. "Avante garde fashion. So hot right now."

She laughs and departs Lyle's world, vanishing like the Cheshire Cat.

Lyle smokes a joint with his roommate to soothe the comedown. Trey is the brooding type who spends his free time convincing people that he spends his free time reading Nietzsche or listening to Elliott Smith with the lights out.

"You're coming to this party with me tonight, right?"

Their apartment is too small and poorly ventilated to support habitual joint smoking, but they do it anyway. Joints just have a classic, old school quality about them, and they live above an off-campus hot spot pizzeria, so they could always just blame the smell on that?

"Unlikely." Trey's got a deep, languid voice that lends his lanky physique a sort of vampiric charm.

"Come on. It'll be quick. Just a business transaction. Maybe a few beers. And I want to meet Erin's new boyfriend."

"Who is it?"

"Davis Radnor?"

"He's back at school?"

"Maybe?"

"Huh. He lived on my floor freshman year. Thought he transferred or something."

"Is he cool?"

"Didn't really know him. His roommates had problems with him, though. I remember that. Something about them fucking with his computer? RAs got involved."

"Do you think he's still living with those guys?"

"No chance. It got pretty ugly if I'm not mistaken."

"So are you coming?"

"Ha. No."

Lyle has to cross campus to get to Crosby Street. It's a solid twenty minute hike from his place in town to the leafier, residential area where the quietness is oppressive, enforced by the very trees themselves. That's the problem with these small liberal arts schools in the New England countryside; once you leave campus you're in the middle of nowhere, a wilderness that rejects your bougie education and hip sensibilities as useless and absurd. A few blocks from here and there's nothing but woods, backwater towns, and highway strip malls for maybe a hundred miles. Lyle, in his hushpuppies and orange paisley bandana headband, is now an oddity, drawing suspicion and scrutiny. He can feel the squirrels' eyes following him like security cameras. Do they know he's got a baggie of weed in his pocket? There is some commotion in the distance; the house glows like a hamlet on a mountainside. His pace quickens and he hurries past the dark, disinterested houses that line the street.

The door is slightly open, and he pushes it timidly. The din of the party grows as he steps inside. Fortunately, the house is crowded and Lyle's entrance doesn't make a scene. He tosses his coat onto the coat pile behind the couch and enthusiastically points at some guy he vaguely recognizes from class, who does not reciprocate the enthusiasm. People who take themselves too seriously are Lyle's preferred source of entertainment, and he gets a great kick out of greeting the stuck up girls in attendance with an exaggerated slack-jawed drawl characteristic of the Sperry-wearing douchebags who are hosting the party. What the fuck is Erin doing schmoozing with these pricks?

"Lyle!"

She is in the hallway leaning against the wall under the shadow of a tall, severe looking guy with a buzz cut. "This is Davis! I'll get you a beer, Lyle." Erin merges with the crowd leaving Lyle and Davis to meet each other.

Davis grips Lyle's hand with a knuckle-racking intensity.

"Watch out for my toe. People have been stepping on my toe."

Lyle wonders for a second if this is some kind of slang, a hip new YouTube reference maybe? But he looks down to check if there is a literal toe in question, and sees that Davis is wearing sandals; the nerdy strapped kind that little kids wear to the beach, or that elderly men wear with socks. This strikes Lyle as disarmingly strange; not only is it March and there are still recalcitrant piles of crusty snow on the ground, but there is nothing to suggest that he is being ironic or whimsical, or that this is simply his eccentric style. Lyle could dig it if he was wearing a Hawaiian shirt or bucket hat or something consciously goofy, but this guy seems strikingly unaware that his footwear is out of place. And his toe is definitely fucked up. The big toe on his right foot is all bloody and the nail looks like it's in danger of falling off.

"Damn. How'd you manage that?"

"I was watching the door and some guys tried to come into the party. Like big meatheads. They were all like "let us in to your fucking party, man" and I was all like "no, fuck you." Then this one guy, he starts pushing me. Asking if I want to fight.

Keeps telling me I'm a pussy. I'm all like "what, you hard, bro? You think you're fucking hard, bro?" And then I push him back. And his boys are all like "you're crazy bro. You're fucking crazy." And then they ran away like little babies. Like little babies."

"Huh." Lyle does not know how to respond.

They look at each other awkwardly.

"Did one of them, like, step on your toe?"

"No. I hit it on the stairs coming back inside."

Erin returns and Lyle starts pounding his beer immediately.

"God, those guys were such assholes," Davis says. "They fucked up my toe."

"Lyle, did you hear some guys tried to beat up Davis? Like who does that?"

"Yeah. Weird. But you live here don't you?" Lyle says, addressing Davis. "Why not just put on a pair of shoes or boots or something?"

"Why?"

"To protect your toe?"

"No, I just don't want people to step on it."

Lyle looks at Erin for some kind of explanation but she is sipping her beer, unfazed by Davis' incoherent train of thought. There is an uncomfortable silence while the three of them look around for nothing in particular.

"Did you want to buy some weed or something?"

"No, fuck that, I don't smoke weed."

"Ok, what is this?" he asks Erin. He is less impatient than he is nervous. The abject strangeness of this interaction, combined with the unfamiliar environment and the intensity of this Davis guy's presence, is inducing a minor freak out. This time, Erin, too, is puzzled. She looks up sweetly at her boyfriend.

"I thought you said you wanted some. For your roommates or something?"

"Yeah."

She breaks her puzzled stare for a split second to glance at Lyle, who's expression has extended from confusion to borderline disgust.

"Do you want to buy some or not?" he demands.

"Fine."

"Fifty bucks for an eighth."

Davis walks away, staring ahead robotically, presumably to get money. Lyle slides in closer to Erin.

"Yo, who is this guy?"

"He's really so sweet. He just needs someone to listen to him."

"And that has to be you?"

"Lyle!" she says as if lightly chastising him. "He's going through some stuff and I want to help him. Wouldn't you help me if I needed it?"

Knowing Erin, she probably does genuinely care about him. Lyle remembers when a blue jay crashed into the window of her dorm room freshman year. She pulled the pillow Lyle was napping on right out from under his head and let the bloody, seizing bird rest on it until it died. Then she buried it in the woods, swaddled in her pillow case in the hopes that it would keep the cats and foxes from finding it.

"Alright, alright."

Just then Davis returns with a fifty dollar bill, which he guile-lessly holds out to Lyle. He thrusts the baggie into Davis' hand, suspecting that this guy is incapable of doing anything suavely.

"I've got to jet," he tells Erin. "Nice to meet you." He nods at Davis who only stares at him in an unfriendly kind of way.

He's almost back to campus when he realizes that, in classic Lyle fashion, he left his coat at the house. It's not too cold, he could probably make it home without it, but if he abandons it now there is no way he will ever see it again.

Crosby street is not totally silent this time. He can hear shouting coming from outside the party house. Sounds pretty vicious, perhaps another 'fight' at the door. It does sound like Davis, he notes, but there doesn't seem to be another pack of bros challenging him. "You selfish bitch," echoes down the street. He's almost jogging to the scene now, fearing the worst when he sees Erin sobbing into her hands while Davis bends over her, screaming at her scalp.

"Leave me alone to talk to that asshole? What was I supposed to say to him? Huh?"

Lyle is not confrontational, never has been. He couldn't be described as aggressive in even the mildest sense. He doesn't even like beer games, or any kind of competition for that matter; imbedded in it is always a kernel of avarice, which Lyle can't bear to see germinate. If it wasn't Erin getting hollered at he would have turned around and waited in the shadows until the kerfuffle resolved itself.

"What the fuck is this," Lyle demands tremulously. He stops a dozen paces away, not about to get in Davis' face. He's gotten his attention regardless. The quiet of Crosby Street is magnified in the absence of Davis' shouting. He twists his neck and stares at Lyle ferociously. Lyle feels his stomach go all prickly and numb and wonders if he's made a mistake. There's no way that this guy is so viciously laying into Erin for leaving him alone with Lyle for a couple minutes, right? In the front yard of all places? It must be Lyle's fried brain misinterpreting confusing stimuli. But then Davis takes a step towards him, his eyes locked.

"Lyle, no!" Erin sobs. "Guys, please!"

"You think you're hard, bro?" Davis says coldly as he takes another step. "You want to fucking go, bro?" He steadily trudges towards Lyle, who steps back wanting to maintain the distance between them. This is a calamitous mistake. If he'd held his ground this whole thing might have fizzled out right there, but instead he let Davis know which one of them was the big dog.

"I'm not gonna fight you, man," still backing up now, "but you can't talk to her like that. That's bullshit."

Davis is right up in Lyle's face, and the look in his eyes is one Lyle's never seen before. His eyes are wide and unflinching as if encased in ice, his brows raised with atavistic anticipation. And they are horribly alive, his eyes, like prisoners raging against the bars of their cell. It seems to Lyle that this man's consciousness is located in his eyeballs rather than his brain. Shoot him in the head and his eyes wouldn't lose their spark, but instead continue staring and scheming.

"Lyle, stop, it's not a big deal!"

"You think you're hard enough to fight me, bro?"

Erin grabs on to Davis' shirt in a vain effort to pull him back, keep him from advancing on Lyle, who's jaw is clamped shut with fear of an imminent beating and fury at his own weakness.

"Davis, come on! Lyle, really, it's ok!"

A window sash slams open across the street,

"Fucking kids!" an old man hollers, "I'm calling the cops!"

Davis whips his head around looking for the old man, but seeing no one, returns his eyes to Lyle this time racked with more conventional-looking rage. "See what you've done!" He grabs Lyle by the shirt and throws him on the grass. He looks up to see Erin dragging a reluctant Davis toward the house. She shakes her head with an apologetic grimace and mouths "I'm sorry."

Lyle spends a good chunk of the next morning lying in bed, reflecting on the events of the previous night. He has to question the accuracy of his recollections; they seem too outlandish. Perhaps his porous memory is confabulating the scene with dreams, imagination, and drug-induced hallucinations. Was that Davis guy really as incoherent as Lyle remembers? Or was the miscommunication on Lyle's part? The sandals, though. And the toe. He couldn't make that shit up. And he definitely knocked Lyle on his ass. The crazy eyes were trippy, though. Like nightmarish. That couldn't have been real.

Lyle hears cereal falling into a bowl. Trey is up, relieving Lyle of his solitude. He walks into the kitchen and feigns a yawn to suggest that he too is just waking up.

"How was the party?"

"Weird, man. Too weird."

"I heard there was a big fight."

"Huh." He pauses for a second, confused, then chases Trey to the couch. "Where'd you hear that?"

"Facebook," he says, sparking up one of the joints he finds in the drawer of the coffee table. "Someone posted on the Campus Confessions page. Got mad likes."

Lyle is familiar with it; a Facebook group where his fellow classmates anonymously post about secret crushes, cheating on tests, jerking off in the dorm shower, etc. Lyle takes a drag of the joint.

"What'd it say?"

"Some bullshit about beating someone up. I didn't read the whole thing."

Lyle grabs his laptop from its charging slot under the couch and hastily navigates to Facebook, the joint dangling from his mouth. Is this post about the toe-jamming kerfuffle? Or maybe it's about the scene he and Erin and Davis made.

"To the little bitch who tried to beat up my friend Davis Radnor last night. You think you can just push people around? Chatting up his girlfriend and telling her lies about him? Well, Davis is one of the best people I know. One of the best guys I've ever met. You want to mess with him I'll fuck you up. You want to step on his toe? I'll break your foot. I'm a football player and I will flatten you if you ever even look at my boy Davis again. What kind of little baby picks a fight with a guy like Davis? He's such a sweet guy even though he's going through a lot right now. You're just drug dealing scum. Try it again, asshole. I'll have you running like the little baby you are."

Lyle senses a major freak out in the works. The pit in his stomach is growing, and the Facebook rant makes less and less sense as he re-reads it compulsively. He interrupts Trey from his Cinnamon Toast Crunch and wordlessly forces him to take the remainder of the joint, most of which Lyle has already sucked down with nervous absentmindedness. Chatting up his girlfriend? Drug-dealing scum? Is this about him? Some kind of warped rumor? Because that is definitely not how it went down, right? Fuck, he shouldn't have smoked that joint. Maybe he's just high and making connections that aren't there. Maybe this is just a drunken rambling and doesn't mean anything and he's just freaking out because he got too high too fast. But, like, fuck! Why couldn't he just wait until he had this figured out before getting high? Now he's going to be all freaked out and confused and unable to think straight for a few hours at the very least. He desperately wants to be un-high right now and just look at this soberly, but he can't. Instead he's trapped in his head, stranded on a tiny, nightmarish island, deliriously thirsty for a cogent thought.

He needs to chill out, he's been through worse. He can totally think his way out of this. He needs to gather more data points. What time was it posted at? 2:38 AM. Who likely posted it? A football player? Lyle doesn't know any football players, so he doubts any know him. Are there any comments? He scrolls down and sees there is only one comment. It is from Davis himself, posted at 2:39 AM.

"Wow, thanks! So great to have so many friends that care about me. Let this be a warning to all the little babies out there who think they're tough."

There's that 'little babies' thing again. What an odd insult. Who says that? It was weird when Davis kept repeating it last night too. Wait a minute. The comment was posted only a minute after the rant. Davis isn't tagged in the post, so the only way he would have seen it immediately is if he happened to be perusing Campus Confessions at 2:38, or if he was in the same room as the football player at the time of the posting, or… if he wrote the rant himself.

Lyle is rapidly losing control of his freak out. He slams his laptop shut and starts pacing around the living room. The sound of Trey's chewing is overwhelming.

"You alright?" Trey asks with his mouth full.

Lyle is breathing heavily. "It's Davis. He wrote it himself. Look at the time stamp."

Trey looks at him skeptically, but Lyle shouts at him to look at it. Trey keeps an eye on Lyle as he opens his laptop and reads the post; he never loses his cool like this. The combination of Facebook nonsense and meatheaded threats should make him crack up, not freak out. Maybe he's finally taken one tab too many. Isn't that how it works? A human brain has x amount of trips in it before short-circuiting, or liquefying, or seizing up like a cramped muscle, or whatever. Nah, probably not. Brains are like, pretty robust, right?

"Dude, chill," he says finally. "He was probably just drunk."

"No, man. No. This guys is off his fucking rocker."

"What even makes you think it's about you. You didn't pick a fight with him, did you?"

"Of course not. But he was like screaming at Erin and I told him to back off. He was the one that tried to start a fight."

Trey listens glassy-eyed as Lyle frantically and semi-coherently recounts the events of the party.

"You need to relax. Here," he says, sifting through the drawer full of pre-rolled joints.

"No! Fuck. I need some air." He stomps into his bedroom to grab his coat, but remembers that it is still at that goddamn house. He clenches his fists and shouts obscenities at the ceiling. Trey is still reclining on the couch, enjoying his cereal, and probably rolling his eyes as Lyle storms out of the apartment. He doesn't react when Lyle tells him he is going to find Erin.

At this time of morning, Erin ought to be in the café on the first floor of the library. She hasn't responded to Lyle's text yet, but flightiness is her MO and she is in the habit of keeping her phone battery in the red. Given that the cafe's lineup of artisanal coffees with seasonal flavors, abundance of power outlets, and hip, bustling energy, it is Erin's natural habitat. Today she is sitting at a table by the window reading a psychology textbook, diligently studying for a test no doubt. She doesn't see Lyle until he slides into the chair opposite her.

"Lyle!" she says beaming with surprise. "What are you doing here?"

"Trying to un-harsh my mellow. What happened last night?"

"Oh, you mean Davis? He got a little riled up."

"No kidding. He looked like he was about to smack you around."

"No," she coos, gently admonishing Lyle. "He's totally harmless. He's actually really sweet."

"Uh-huh. Did you see what he wrote on the Campus Confessions page?"

"He told me about it. Something about his boys having his back?"

"His boys? Are you shitting me? Erin, this guy is out of his head. If I didn't know any better I'd think he just transferred from the Laughing Academy."

"Lyle!" She's got her frowny face on now. "Mental health is not something to joke about."

"Sorry, not a psychology major like you." Erin folds her arms and Lyle knows he might actually be in trouble. He suddenly feels terrible and all the tension oozes out of his body. "Look, I'm sorry. I'm kind of freaked out. This guy is scaring me a little bit."

"I think maybe he felt threatened by you. Davis can be unpredictable, but he's a person all the same and deserves the patience and respect you would show anyone else. Maybe you should apologize to him."

"Apologize? For what! I didn't do anything."

"Just let him know that you don't want any misunderstandings and that you want to start over on the right foot."

Lyle resists decrying her idea as bullshit. Instead, he looks at her softly and wishes he could just hug her tightly until he is no longer scared and she is no longer annoyed.

"Fine."

"Go to his house around four. He should be back by then. I'll let him know you're coming." She closes her textbook and starts packing up. "I've got to get to class." She buckles up her leather backpack and before walking away says, "Go easy on him, Lyle. He really is a nice guy."

It has been raining on and off all day. Lyle can't decide if the air is exceptionally damp, or if it is raining extremely lightly. The fact that it could be both blows his mind. Or maybe the moisture produced by the faintly melting snow in the barely above-freezing temperatures is rising like... upside down rain? Far out. Lyle skipped his one class today on account of needing to chill out in a big way, and he spent most of the afternoon smoking weed with Trey and watching *Ancient Aliens* to like, steady his nerves. He chalked up his early morning freak out to not being a morning person and dropping a fat tab of acid the day before. He remembered that weed is good for anxiety and the like. He also decided to be at his mellowest for this majorly stressful apology session. He'd rather smell like weed than fear.

The sky is a thick, milky gray and the wispy clouds swirl languidly like smoke in a bong. The cold air makes Lyle's nose run. He is walking briskly with his head down, as he unconsciously does when really high to avoid narc-related red eye detection, but also because Crosby Street gives him the heebie-jeebies. He wants to get this over and done with. In his mind this will be a quick, We Cool? Yeah, We Cool-type conversation that won't go any further than the front door, or any longer than thirty seconds. The wooden steps and porch creak painfully as he approaches the door. He knocks.

Davis answers the door stone faced, his eyes seem to be staring blindly above and beyond Lyle's head.

"Hey man, I just wanted to come by and say – "

"Let's take a walk." The words are terse and authoritative. Before Lyle can muster the words to object, Davis is putting on a jacket. Lyle's jacket. He's unsure if he should say something – this is not a time for confrontation – but, like, it's his jacket.

"Is that my jacket?" he asks tepidly as Davis walks past him and down the stairs of the porch. Lyle has to semi-jog to keep up.

"No," Davis says, his eyes ahead. "Someone left this at the party last night. I found it this morning."

"Yeah," cautiously now, "I think I'm the one who left it."

Lyle simply can't walk as fast as Davis. He must look like an idiot having to hop-skip-jump every few steps just to keep up. It doesn't seem to Lyle as if Davis is being a dick about the jacket, or ignoring Lyle, more like he just didn't hear what he said.

"How long have you known Erin?"

Lyle notices that they are walking away from campus and towards the woods. This is all happening really fast. Like, so fast he can't stop it – their unsettling trajectory, Davis' weirdness, his rising sense of claustrophobic panic. He feels wildly out of control, and it doesn't help that he's too high to have a firm grip on his thoughts; they, too, are moving too fast, and pinning one of them down is like trying to grasp slippery fish right out of the water.

"Uh." Why is he asking questions? What the fuck is happening? "Did Erin tell you why I was coming over? I just wanted to, like, make sure there was no beef between us, or whatever."

"I don't trust her. I don't trust her at all." They turn off the sidewalk and onto a dirt trail. Lyle recognizes it as the bike path to the reservoir, a popular place to drink and do drugs when the weather is nice. "I think she's lying to me."

"What? No," Lyle says in soothing tones. "What makes you say that?"

"I've seen her talking to my roommates. They're planning something. I think they want me out of the house. They're trying to get me kicked out of school."

There is no longer any doubt as far as Lyle is concerned; this man is totally fucking out of his head. Worse, he's mentally ill. Adjectives like insane and crazy seem wholly inappropriate; this guy is clearly unwell in a clinical way. Lyle suddenly senses how important it is that he treat this man cautiously. Speak softly and affirmatively. Going against the grain could be calamitous, and there is no way out of this conversation. They're straight up in the woods now; the residential neighborhood has disappeared behind the tight lattice of leafless tree branches, and there is no human presence out here. No dog walkers or joggers or bird-watchers. No one to, like, hear him scream.

"You're not getting along with your roommates?"

"They're scheming something. I know it. Last weekend, at The White Horse, they were pointing at me across the bar. Pointing their fingers like guns, like they're letting me know I'm finished. Like they've got a hit out on me or something."

"Are you, um. Do you, like, know them super well?"

"I went to high school with two of them. They were cool, but Erin's changed them."

Davis stops abruptly. They are on a short bridge that crosses over a partially frozen canal. He leans on his elbows on the damp cobblestone and stares off into the distance at the reservoir.

"Oh yeah? How's that?"

"She's trying to ruin my life, I know it. I don't know how well you think you know her, but you can't trust her. She's trying to destroy my life so she can fuck all my roommates. She used me to get to them and now she doesn't need me anymore and wants me out of the picture."

"I uh. I don't think that's –"

"You don't know her like I know her. She's insane. Some kind of sexual deviant. And a drug addict. My roommates are all drug addicts and they want to have these fucked up druggie orgies in the basement with Erin. That's why I had to buy the weed. Keep them from getting suspicious of me. I have to blend in to bide my time."

Lyle's got that hot, prickly feeling surging up his neck and enveloping his scalp and face. He looks around frantically for, like, options? But there are none. This guy is utterly delusional, paranoid, sick. Completely unpredictable. What if he suddenly thinks Lyle is like their spy or some shit and decides he needs to neutralize him? Chop him up and bury him in the woods and so forth. But if he makes a run for it, Davis might think he's off to tell Erin and her BDSM gang, or whatever, and go to her house and bludgeon her to death, or something.

"I, uh. Hm. I've got nothing to do with any of this." His voice is shaking.

"I know. You're all right. I can tell. She's trying to ruin your life, too. Maybe she's already ruined yours. That's what she does, she ruins a guy's life and moves on to her next victim. We need to have each other's backs. That's why I brought you out here, I didn't want anyone to see us or let Erin or my roommates know that we're working together."

Lyle is shocked speechless. He is silent for long enough that Davis looks at him and forces eye contact. Lyle gets the uncanny and frighteningly intense sensation of being far, far from home. The monotonous rushing of the canal under him has turned into an intolerable drone like a Sunday morning leaf blower, growing louder and louder until Lyle feels the need to shout at it to shut the fuck up. He wishes desperately that he wasn't high. A robin taking off makes him flinch.

"Maybe you should just break up with her. Like, never talk to her again. Don't let her ruin your life and just put the whole thing behind you."

"No. I have to see this through. I'm not going to let her or my roommates get away with this. Let them get away with picking on the depressed kid? That's fucked up. No way."

Lyle pulls out his phone and looks at the time. "Hey, so, I have to go. Got this study group thing." He takes a few steps backwards. "We cool?"

"Yeah, we're cool. You've got my back, right?"

"Yeah. Of course." Lyle turns and speed-walks back down the path. He looks over his shoulder every few steps, making sure that Davis is still on the bridge, watching the icy water meander home.

When Lyle returns to his apartment he collapses on the couch. He sits silently, but the silence is not altogether contemplative. Rather, he lets himself slip into coma-like rumination. He feels shitty, physically and otherwise. The warmth of his apartment thaws him out, leaving him with a numb, fuzzy, feverish feeling. A harsh comedown, replete with headache and dry mouth, does not help. Not to mention he is terrified, genuinely fearing for his life for perhaps the first time. Davis is so out of touch with reality, so unpredictable and deliriously frightened, that the thought of him doing something heinous and incomprehensible is not farfetched. Lyle, too, is now wrapped up in Davis' paranoid delirium, a character in his dark twisted narrative, a patron at his mad tea party, and there is no escape. This school, this town, is too small to avoid him indefinitely, especially if Davis wants to find him. He's trapped with a madman, and so is Erin. Does she realize the danger she is in? He has to call her.

"Lyle?" She is evidently in the middle of something, walking somewhere.

"Erin," he blurts out, "you have to stop seeing that guy. He's out of his head. Completely. I think he's going to –"

"Slow down, I can't hear you. Did you go over to talk to him today?"

"Yeah, and it was the fucking weirdest half hour of my life. He took me for a walk in the woods and told me all sorts of insane shit. Like, about how you're scheming to kill him and elope with his roommates or something. It didn't make any sense. And he was wearing my jacket. Like, he stole my jacket and doesn't even know it. And something about you being a drug addict and a sexual deviant."

"Lyle, stop." She's exasperated. "I get that you don't like him, or understand him, but this isn't ok."

"Jesus Christ, Erin. This guy is dangerous. Like, I know you want to help him or fix him or whatever, but he's not a goddamn blue jay with a broken neck. He needs real help. You can't mommy him back to health."

Lyle hears her take a deep breath. She wants to be sweet and gentle, she knows that Lyle is probably just jealous or bitter or something, but her voice comes out all strained like Play-Doh being cranked through a toy spaghetti maker. "You don't know what you're talking about."

"You're being naïve and you're going to get hurt. You're just confusing him more. There's a reason therapists don't sleep with their patients."

"Oh, fuck you, Lyle. Maybe you're the one losing touch with reality." There's a pause, and her voice softens. "I'm sorry. I have to go."

She hangs up the phone without waiting for a response.

Lyle huffs and puffs and walks around the living room. Maybe he's the one losing touch with reality? Bullshit. As if this is some M. Night Shyamalan movie. As if it's all in his head, or Davis is actually Lyle's split personality, or he's been on Shutter Island the entire goddamn time. Suddenly every psychological thriller he's ever watched seems beyond stupid. Real-life mental illness, it turns out, is far scarier than any trite plot twist.

He hears someone at the door, jostling with the handle. He freezes.

Trey stops short in the doorway, alarmed by the Raskolnikov-looking character in his living room. "What's up?"

Lyle launches into the events of the afternoon while Trey walks cautiously to the couch. He doesn't take his eyes off Lyle.

"Huh." There's a hint of incredulity in his voice. "Sounds pretty fucked, man. Sorry you had to deal with that."

"You know the guy, right? Should I be worried?"

"I don't know him. He just lived in my dorm freshman year. You should talk to his old roommates, though."

"Who did he live with?"

"He was in the quad in the basement. I want to say one of them was named Derek."

"Derek Goldstein?"

"Yeah, that sounds right. Portly bearded guy."

Lyle, still dressed for the outdoors, darts out of the apartment without another word.

It's dark outside. The streetlights are on. Already a line is forming in the pizzeria. Derek lives nearby in a slovenly house with half a dozen roommates. Lyle's been there before, mostly to work on computer programming projects and assignments, but also to buy or trade hard-to-get drugs.

"Wassup Lyle." One of Derek's similarly bearded housemates answers the door. "Tell me you've got some Scooby Snacks for us."

"Not tonight, amigo. I need to talk to Derek."

The amigo leads Lyle into the house and up the stairs, from where he can already hear the ruckus and clanging steel of cinematic carnage. Derek is lounging on a beanbag chair in front of a wall-sized projection of *Game of Thrones* beaming from a craftily wired ceiling projector. The room is dark like a theater, illuminated only by the eerie glow of the projection. Derek pauses on a frame of a furious dragon baring fangs and flaring nostrils.

"Lyle, man. What brings you to my lair this evening?"

"I need some intel."

"My leads are all dry at the moment I'm afraid. Feds are cracking down on the TOR network. Shoring things up around here."

"I hear you, man." Lyle takes a seat in an ergonomic gaming chair and instinctively grips the joysticks on the arm rests. "But do you know a guy named Davis Radnor?"

Derek eyes Lyle and reaches for a bong worth, Lyle estimates, upwards of 400 dollars. "Yeah I know him." Lyle watches the white smoke swirl as Derek pulls it up through ice chambers and honeycomb percolators to deliver a perfect hit.

"I sold him weed last night and shit's getting weird for me now."

Derek, coughing and sputtering on his monster hit, chokes out: "you sold that dude weed!" The smoke rises in front of the projector, which makes for a groovy, noir effect. "That is one motherfucker who should not be altering his consciousness."

"How's that?" Lyle accepts the bong and rips it hard. He exhales up into the eye of the projector and wonders if he should really be smoking right now, but doesn't push the question.

Derek groans and scratches his beard. "It's a long fucking story."

"I've got a long story of my own. I need your help, man. Trey told me you'd been through something similar."

"I hope not, dude. If you're in it that deep with him you better lawyer-up or some shit."

"Oh Christ. What happened?"

"Basically he had some kind of bipolar episode. Nothing was ever explained to us but that's the best I can deduce. Anyway, he was one of my roommates freshman year. I was in a quad with him, Terry McClean and Joey Nussbaum. You know those guys? Anyway, it was all cool for most of the year. We got along. Me and Joey were homies, still are, and Terry's cool I guess. Davis was, like, a really swag dude, though. Good looking guy, you know? He operated in a different social sphere than the rest of us. He's from some ritzy Boston suburb and had a bunch of friends from prep school who he'd chill with most of the time. He always bought expensive alcohol, wore really nice clothes. He would wear a fucking blazer to go out. But towards the end of the year he started going on about us hacking his Facebook. Because we were like computer geeks or something? I don't know, but he kept accusing us of messing with his profile, reading his private messages, talking shit about him on Twitter. And none of us ever touched his shit. Ever. And there wasn't anything ostensibly weird about his Facebook neither. It's not like someone was posting bullshit or anything. He thought we were hacking onto his Facebook and, like, just looking around? Spying on him? I don't know. But then he starts posting all sorts of weird shit himself – rants, weird comments on girls' photos – and he blames that on us. He found me in the library one day and started screaming at me, like really screaming, and made this whole scene, saying that I was trying to ruin his life."

"I've heard that one."

"Yeah. Well, I still had to live with this guy. And I started to really fucking hate him. Like really hate him. Maybe the only time I've ever seriously hated anyone." Lyle can tell Derek is getting riled up. He passes him the bong and lighter, and waits for him to take another rip.

"Where was I?"

"You really hated him."

"Yeah. Jesus. What an awful feeling. True hate. I couldn't sleep because I hated him so much. I'd lay in bed, kind of too scared to go to sleep because that crazy asshole was sleeping six feet away from me. God, what a scene. All four of us, laying in the dark, pretending to be asleep, spazzing at any little sound.

Davis was scared too. More scared than us, even. He must have really believed we were out to get him. And this went on for a few days. None of us slept for at least four days. I'd sneak a nap in the library or something, but shit, we must have all looked like maniacs. I couldn't focus or enjoy anything. I was totally consumed with this tight feeling in my gut, like my stomach was all wrung out like a sponge. I just wanted him out of my life. I wanted him to disappear. To cease existing."

He pauses for a minute, so absorbed in his train of thought that he seems to have forgotten that he is holding the bong.

"And you know what I learned? People think that hate is the opposite of love. It's not. Hate is the opposite of safety. Like, hate is just an evolutionary response to feeling threatened. It prepares you emotionally to neutralize a threat. It's an extension of the fight-or-flight complex. Without hate we never would have had it in us to spear saber-toothed tigers that cornered us in our caves, or hunt down the packs of wolves that snatched our babies out of our camps. We would have just run away like deer and never have advanced as a species. Fear and hate, man. The true impetus for our evolution."

Lyle sinks deeper into the plush gaming chair and he finds that he cannot look away from the opal eyes of the dragon glaring down at him. It is frozen fractions of a second before incinerating Lyle in a typhoon of flame and rage. He takes the bong back from Derek and, eyes still fixed on the dragon, sparks up.

"Anyway. One day me, Terry, and Joey come back from dinner to find all our laptops broken in half. Like, the monitors have all been separated from the keyboards. The wires are all hanging out and shit. The glass was all broken because they'd been stomped on. And he'd arranged them on our pillows like those severed horse heads in *The Godfather*."

"Goddamn."

Derek laughs percussively. "Just wait. It gets worse. We're all stewing, furious, about to kill this guy. Like, go feral on him. Foaming at the mouth type shit. Joey goes to tell the RA, but when he opens the door Davis is just standing there, like waiting for him. I guess Joey lunged at him or something, but Davis grabbed him by the shirt and threw him into the wall. The thud was loud enough to get people to poke their heads out of their rooms. It was totally silent for a second, but then Joey threw up, like projectile vomited from his concussion, *Exorcist* style, all over the hallway." Derek starts laughing, cracking up even, pinching the bridge of his nose to keep his glasses on his face. "You wouldn't believe how much he threw up, man! I've never seen anything like it!"

Lyle nervously joins in on the laughter. His eyes dart between Derek and the dragon as if he doesn't want either of them to catch him with his back turned. He breaks up Derek's laughing fit. "So what happened next?"

"Sorry," he says, calming down. "Terry and I both jump him and it's this whole scene. Ripping clothes, pulling hair, mashing faces into the ground, crotch shots, you name it."

"And no one came out to help you guys?"

"Of course not! Ha! And get written up for fighting? Or get a rogue elbow to the face? Or step in Joey's barf? No way, they were smart not to. Don't ever get involved with lunatics. Trying to help will only get you in trouble. If you see a shit storm coming your way, pull your hood up and batten down the hatches. But I don't need to tell you that." Derek grins and Lyle gets impatient.

"Come on, man. Who won the fight?"

"No one ever wins a fight like that, man. Two RAs came running down the hallway, keys jangling on their lanyards like sirens. They pulled us off each other and separated us. I actually burst a blood vessel in my eye I was screaming so loud. Like, incoherent nonsense. Mostly just grunts and spit. And you know me. I'm not a wild guy at all. I literally lost my mind. Like, I blacked out. It was like being ravenous with hunger and ripping into a fresh kill without having the presence of mind to filet it or cook it or anything. That's how much I hated him."

"Did you get in trouble?"

"Something like that. Campus PD already had three squad cars and an ambulance outside the dorm by the time they were able to drag us out the door. Joey went to health services and the rest of us got taken to separate rooms in the main administration building. The same place you have to go to turn in those bullshit essays when you get written up for drinking. Anyway, two ladies came and took my deposition or whatever. One was the dean of student conduct and the other was a counselor. Asked me about my feelings and stuff. I tried telling them that Davis was sick in the head and needed counseling or medication or something, but they more or less ignored me. Long story short, Terry and I had to spend the night in the infirmary with Joey and some bozo who couldn't hold his booze. When we were allowed to go back to our room in the morning his stuff was all gone. Bed was stripped and everything."

"Just like that? He was gone?"

"Apparently his mom drove up with two lawyers and made a scene. Other kids in the dorm told us that the lawyers hollered at the RAs while his mom helped Davis move all of his stuff out. And get this. Two days later she came back and gave each of us two thousand bucks for the laptops on the condition that we didn't file any complaints or press charges."

"Wow. So he didn't finish the semester or anything?"

"Not that I know of. My best guess is that his mom made some kind of deal with the university. I'll bet she threatened some kind of heavy duty litigation and the university didn't want any trouble, so they just pretended it never happened. Terry and I didn't even get written up after all that. We just got an email asking us not to talk about it."

"So why the shit is he back here?"

"Ha. Excellent question. I'll bet the Radnor estate made a fat donation and safety-pinned a doctor's note to his shirt. I got an email in September saying he would be back on campus and that he had a restraining order against me. So when I see him I turn around and walk the other way. I advise you do the same from here on out."

Lyle can pretty much hear his hands un-sticking as he lets go of the joysticks, which, he realizes, he has been gripping with white-knuckle intensity for some time. Derek angles a remote control so that the buttons are illuminated by the light of the projector. "And if you somehow get me involved with Davis Radnor again" – he un-pauses the screen and the room shakes with the dragon's roar and the screams of knights being incinerated by its breath – "I'll fucking kill you."

Lyle nearly falls out the chair with fright when the show restarts. He inelegantly makes it look like he was standing up to leave.

"Want to watch *Game of Thrones?*" Derek asks.

"I've got to go. Thanks for the intel, man. I owe you one."

"Like I said, man. Pull your hood up and batten down the hatches."

Lyle has to blink a lot while walking back to his apartment. He got way higher than he thought. Expensive bongs will do that. The cylinders of acrid yellow light beaming down from the street lights look like solid cones of gold to Lyle, who is afraid to look at the ground they are illuminating for fear of seeing a ferocious dragon projected on the sidewalk. He can't really feel his legs and only knows he's walking because the line snaking out of the pizzeria is getting closer. It's not unusual for the line to meander down the sidewalk at this time of night, given that it is the only by-slice-pizza joint in town. He squints to make sure he's not hallucinating. There's no way that that's Davis, some fifty feet away, standing in line with his prep-school housemates. No fucking way. Davis turns his head robotically and makes piercing eye contact with Lyle, who trips over his own feet as he comes to a jarring stop. He can feel that Davis is still staring at him and, in a desperate move, steps off the curb without looking. A car screeches to a halt and honks at him. Lyle looks around, a deer in the headlights, and sees that the whole line is now looking at him. He regains his situational awareness and jogs the rest of the way across the street. Now what? The door to his apartment building is right next to the pizzeria, right on the other side of the line. Maybe if he times it right he can cross back over once Davis is inside. He puts his hood up and saunters to the end of the block and then turns around again hoping that this has bought him enough time. He darts across the street, looking this time, and fumbles for his keys. He's too jittery for the steady-handedness required to fit a key into a lock and he bumbles at the door for just a second too long. Davis steps out of the pizzeria with a slice on a paper plate in his hand. They definitely see each other.

Lyle pretty much falls across the threshold and runs up the two floors to his apartment and bolts the door behind him. Trey isn't home, and Lyle is too agitated to flop down on the couch. He walks around in circles to use up the excess electricity in his muscles. Jesus, what just happened? He almost got hit by a car, skulked up and down the block with his hood up like some kind of shady, cloaked villain, ran through his apartment like he was being chased, and now he's pacing in tight circles around his living room. Did he even see Davis? Was that really him? In retrospect, maybe not, he was pretty far away. This doesn't look good, he realizes. Anyone observing Lyle objectively would deduce that he is crazy. His behavior is abnormal. Dangerously so? Maybe he should smoke a quick bowl to mellow him out. Wait, what? How could that possibly be his first thought? He's unreasonably high as it is. Logical reasoning would draw a connection between a major bong session and his erratic behavior. Shit. Does Lyle have a drug problem? Like an honest-to-God substance abuse problem? He's admitted it himself: he loves weed. He's even said that he loves weed like a woman, like the only girlfriend that ever really understood him. He keeps wanting to go back for more even though he knows on some subconscious level that he shouldn't. Maybe it's not even a subconscious level. Maybe the green spirit that's possessed him just speaks louder than his own consciousness and has suppressed his own free will. But not like violently suppressed it, like hardcore addiction might. More like lulled it into submission. Maybe Mary Jane has deceived Lyle, with soothing tones and whimsical charisma, into thinking that her voice is actually his. Is that it's evolutionary advantage? Rather than offer tasty fruit to encourage animals to spread its seeds and cultivate it, it uses sly deception. Rather than offering nourishment, it provides the pleasurable illusion that things are different, funnier, more thrilling, more positive, when in fact, nothing has actually changed. It makes your thoughts sound different, more profound, more intriguing, even though you might have had the exact same train of thought sober. It makes you feel a little more optimistic by seducing you into thinking that things are going to work out, that things are in fact more beautiful than you had previously realized, stripping away the layers of earthly bullshit to reveal the Platonic ideals of everything around you. This is when the plant tightens its tendrils. Your reflection starts to look a little better in the mirror. Mary Jane whispers in your ear: you shouldn't be so hard on yourself, you're actually doing all right, everything is going to be totally groovy. Whatever it is you need to do, you can do it no problem. So you might as well just kick back, smoke a joint, indulge yourself. Suddenly Mary Jane's convinced you that she is fundamentally good. What could possibly be bad about a plant that reveals a brighter beauty and vivacity in the world? How can something that makes music sound this good possibly be bad? Next thing you know, you're starting to believe the articles online that say that THC cures cancer, that marijuana roots revitalize damaged soil, that all the great minds of history dabbled with the good leaf. Then you reason that there is no way marijuana is just a plant like any other; its properties are too remarkable. It's the very spirit of Mother Earth herself sprouting from the ground, a conduit to merge your consciousness with hers. Now that you are fully ready to embrace the glory of the Green Spirit, you tell Mary Jane, while you're on a date in the park, watching the sun bleed into the sky, that you trust her completely. That you'll love her forever. But unlike a true lover, she uses this power over you to her advantage. She tells you she loves you back, when really she's just using you to spread her seeds and influence.

What a bunch of paranoid shit. Lyle needs to get a hold of himself. Anthropomorphic plants? Jesus, he must be really high. Wait, but what if those aren't his own thoughts? What if that is Mary Jane again, masquerading as reason, working damage control? Why would he try to convince himself that a drug is good? Why would he force himself to ignore the side effects, reject any negative observations? He knows in a vague way that hallucinogens can cause paranoia, confusion, memory loss etc. He knows that a strong affinity for marijuana is correlated to latent schizophrenia, and that smoking weed exacerbates predispositions for mental illness. But he always seems to ignore that. Whether Mary Jane or Lyle himself is the great deceiver is irrelevant. Lyle is so tightly wrapped up in the deception that he can no longer trust his thoughts to ascertain any kind of objective reality. Will he ever know what's real again? Will he just drift in paranoid limbo forever? Is he doomed to hobble hunched over, shivering with fear, hugging himself for some desperately needed security, through the dark recesses of fear and loathing for all eternity?

He can't calm himself down. He can't shut it off. He's lost control of his mind; legions of anxiety and panic have stormed the throne room and usurped his feeble consciousness. He starts breathing heavily, his heart is beating so fast that it starts palpitating. Stumbling and shaking, he barges into his room and rifles clumsily through his drug dealing safe. He plucks out a blue pill, which he knows to be the last of the Xanax he got from Derek. He throws it down his gullet and curls up as tightly as he can under his blankets. Soon enough, his mind slows and he dissolves into the darkness.

Lyle wakes up some twelve hours later to find six missed calls and two text messages from Erin.

"Are you ok?"

"Meet me at the café as soon as you get this."

His head might as well be full of lint, and his muscles require more effort than usual to work, sort of like being underwater. He reflects on his Category 5 freak out last night, but gives up before thinking about it critically. Six missed calls is a lot, though. In the early hours of the morning no less.

Lyle gets up and waits for a blinding head rush to pass. He stretches out with quivering feline intensity and decides the best way to describe his overall physical and emotional state is 'pleasantly subdued.'

On the way to campus he realizes he forgot his backpack, which strikes him as comically preposterous. It's only upon passing the café that he remembers why his feet have brought him there. Erin presumably has something urgent to say to him. His response will be something along the lines of 'don't come near me until you're done with that Davis guy,' and then walk out without ever having sat down. That is, until he sees that she has been crying. Her face is blotchy and red, and she sniffles and hiccups pitifully at regular intervals.

"What's going on?" he asks seriously.

She merely holds up her phone and shows him a text conversation with Davis. Mostly capital letters, obscenities, exclamation marks. "Why aren't you answering my calls?" type stuff. He scrolls down, and down, and down some more. The stream of texts are endless, coming every minute or so for several hours. There are literally hundreds of them from 11 at night all the way until 6 AM. There is an occasional text bubble from Erin pleading with him to calm down, but every time she responds Davis doubles down on the verbal abuse and violence. At one point, Lyle spots his name.

"Answer or so help me I will fuck up Lyle's day." This is followed by a stream of vitriol, including threats to break all his teeth, break all his bones, set him on fire, and so forth. And then, finally, "I know he lives above the pizzeria. I saw him there last night. Pick up your phone or I swear to God I will go in there and kill him in his sleep." So ends the onslaught of text messages. Erin evidently took him seriously enough to call him back.

"So you called the cops and they arrested him, right?"

Erin takes her phone back and hides it in her pocket. "We went to couples counseling in health services this morning."

Lyle can't help but laugh. "Couples counseling! Now I've heard everything." He is more angry than frightened. Or maybe so frightened he's angry.

"You don't understand. If he gets in trouble, he'll get kicked out of school forever."

"Un. Fucking. Believable. You're willing to risk your life, and mine too by the way, so that this guy can, what? Get a diploma? Do you know what he did freshman year?"

"Yes. But he took a year off and got help and medication."

"Doesn't seem to have done him much good."

"They're just trying to rebalance his medicine. He just needs time. If he has another episode he'll have to be institutionalized. He'll be barred from the university. He'll never be able to get a job. The stigma will follow him for the rest of his life."

"Not my fault."

"Did Davis send you anything?"

"Like a letter bomb?"

"Like on Facebook."

"I haven't checked. Why?"

"He told the couples counselor that he sent you a message."

Without another word Lyle slides Erin's laptop in front of him and logs into Facebook. One new message.

"How could you do this to me? You traitor. You fucking traitor! You said you had my back. You're just as bad as the rest of them, you lying piece of shit. Telling my girlfriend lies to get her to break up with me? You were working with them all along. How could I have been so blind. I'll get you for this. I know you've got a bunch of drugs in your apartment. Maybe I'll call the campus police with an anonymous tip. I'm sure they'll find a bunch of interesting stuff. I'll come visit you in prison, you fuck."

Lyle closes the laptop slowly. He's got that thousand-mile stare that sees nothing. There's enough weed and acid in his apartment to land him in prison. Big time. He envisions barbed wire, orange jumpsuits, lace-less shoes, two-way mirrors, damp concrete walls, smirking, tattooed faces, and steel jawed correctional officers slowly slapping batons on their open palms. He can just about hear the deafening buzz signaling the mechanized opening of a steel door, the rest of his life slowly revealing itself on the smooth, gray concrete on the other side. He might actually shit himself right there in the café.

"My life is over."

"What?" Erin is alarmed.

"I'm fucked. The cops are probably over there right now. I didn't even close my safe last night. It's over."

He stands up and starts to walk away, his eyes still not fixed on anything in particular. Erin stands too and tries to grab him from across the table, but misses. She trips over chair legs and backpacks as she tries to reach after him.

She shouts, "Lyle, we have to go to the Dean. He –"

Lyle tears himself from her grip, scowls and says something hateful before storming off in the direction of his apartment. He's vaguely aware that Erin is crying and that he himself is exiting stage left of a major scene in the works. Even the baristas are paying attention now.

Shortly after getting off campus he realizes he needs to run. He might still have time. The cold air singes his lunges. Snow is starting to fall and Lyle slides around corners with reckless abandon. He barges into his apartment, expecting it to be torn apart by a rapacious search and seizure operation. But there is nothing. The space has never felt so still. He's never noticed the clock tick before, and wow does it tick loudly. The half eaten bowl of cereal seems contrived, a tensely plotted objet d'art. No cops yet, but what if they've been staking out his apartment, waiting for him to return, hoping they could get him to open the door, sleaze their way in, and then bust him right then and there. He squats low and pulls his hair, and screams silently into the ground. He dead bolts the door and jams one of the kitchen chairs under the knob. He strides back and forth thinking about what to do next. The apartment reeks of weed; flat and stale like bong water. If the cops smell that they'll have probable cause. They'll make him sit on the couch and watch while they go through his stuff, don latex gloves to examine with exaggerated suspicion everything he owns, and then smugly say "well, well, well" as they dangle his stash in front of his face. They'll force eye contact and smirk while they announce into their radios that they've successfully apprehended the perpetrator.

He races into the bathroom, knocking a bunch of toiletries off the sink as he grabs the Febreeze. He unloads the entire can in the living room and hallway. The air is wet with the laundry scented mist. But it isn't enough. He goes into the kitchen area and falls to his knees, sticking half his body into the under-sink space where industrial cleaners are kept. Before even standing up, he mashes down the aerosol tip of an enormous can of Raid and walks around his apartment with his spraying arm outstretched as if confronting a vampire with a crucifix.

He starts coughing violently and drops the can of Raid before stumbling into his bedroom. His drug dealing safe, a steel box disguised as a dictionary, is laying open on top of his dresser. There is something horribly vulgar about the image of the open safe, its illicit innards garishly exposed. To Lyle, it might as well be a naked corpse left splayed at a murder scene. His initial instinct is to slam it shut, but he's in such a hurry that he knocks his dresser, sending the safe and its scattered contents to the floor. A Ziploc bag with over an ounce of glistening nugs spills onto the carpet, and a sheet of acid the size of an index card, 64 tabs in all, each stamped with Scooby-Doo's face and slobbery tongue, floats under his bed, cutting through the air like an errant paper plane.

There is a knock on the apartment door. He yelps audibly and clumsily gathers the weed back into its baggie. The knocking is now a banging, and he reaches under his bed and grabs the sheet of acid with his bare hands.

"Lyle?" It's Trey. "Open the door, man." He's rattling the door violently. "What the fuck is this?"

In an unprecedented moment of peace and stillness, Lyle ogles the baggie of weed and LSD tabs. He knows he should just flush it all down the toilet but... he can't. The heat will die down eventually and he'll wish he had his stash. He could, of course, just buy more later, but, like, what a waste. What a tragic loss that would be, those gorgeous nugs, that top-notch acid. He doesn't have it in him to send them swirling into the sewers. Mary Jane deserves better than that. He stuffs it into his backpack and swings it over his shoulder.

"Coming! Jesus!"

The door handle continues to jiggle. Lyle removes the chair and slides the deadbolt. The door swings open so fast that he doesn't have time to move his hand out of the way. He recoils and shouts an expletive. Trey pushes past him into the apartment and grimaces with disgust.

"What the shit is that *smell?*" He covers his nose and mouth with his sleeve. His eyes are clamped shut and he coughs with gagging intensity. Lyle, meanwhile, is squatting low in the corner, moaning over his bloody knuckles.

"You motherfucker!" he shrieks. He stands up and gets in Trey's face. "You fucked up my hand!"

"Fuck you, you fucked up my apartment." Trey picks up the can of Raid off the kitchen tiles. "Jesus Christ, dude. Are you on some kind of bad trip?"

"The cops are coming. Davis told them about my stash." He suddenly remembers the joints in the three-legged coffee table and strides across the hallway into the living room.

Trey pauses and talks to him from the kitchen. "Ok man. Let's go get some air or some pizza or something."

Lyle bounds back into the kitchen with a fist full of joints and thrusts them on to Trey, who receives them patiently.

"Lyle, man, I think you're freaking out. The cops aren't coming."

"Please Trey, you have to believe me." Lyle is grabbing Trey's shirt and grievously breaching his personal space. The eye contact is sustained, and whatever Trey sees prompts him to rip his shirt from Lyle's grip.

"Did you get something new from Derek today?"

"No, man. No. Davis Radnor. He thinks I'm trying to like sabotage him or something. He's trying to neutralize me by getting me arrested."

"Huh. How about that."

"You don't believe me?"

"We should go for a walk or something."

"No!" Lyle's reaction is explosive and wholly unexpected. He backs up, panic stricken, towards the door. The last person to take him for a walk was Davis. "Hide those joints, man. They're coming." He closes the door, keeping his eyes on Trey, and then turns to head down the stairs. If Trey won't believe him, Derek will.

Lyle scans the sidewalk before exiting the building. No cops, no Davis. But that black sedan could be one of those undercover deals. There's no one in it, though. He should make a break for it while they're getting coffee or asking the neighbors for intel. He peels his forehead off the window and does his best to go incognito. Hood up, eyes down. There is already a thin accumulation of snow on the ground. He will leave tracks. He starts walking with a skating sort of gait to obscure the treads of his hushpuppies. If he can just get a couple blocks to Derek's house and ditch his stash, he'll be home free.

Lyle turns off of the main street and can see Derek's house. The wet snow gives it an especially slovenly and haunted sort of look. He's never noticed how chipped the paint on the door is. In fact, when he knocks, he realizes that one of the hinges is loose and the door hangs crooked, never closing completely.

"Lyle, compadre, what's up?"

One of Derek's homies. Is it possible that Lyle never learned any of their names?

"I've gotta see Derek."

"I think he's in the shower."

Lyle brushes past the homie and takes the stairs up to Derek's lair two at a time. He sees steam slithering out from underneath yet another crooked door.

"Derek!" He bangs on the door. "You in there?"

Pipes squeal as the shower's hiss stops abruptly. Lyle listens to the subtle commotion of a towel whipping off a hook, errant drips echoing in the shower, and the slap of wet feet on tile. The door opens.

"Lyle? What are you doing here, man?" Derek looks strangely mammalian; he carries more blubber and hair on his abdomen than Lyle had previously noted.

"Dude, I've gotta ditch my stash." Lyle swings his backpack off and starts digging around in the main compartment. He lets out a shrill, breathless obscenity when he realizes that he didn't seal the baggie. There are crushed nugs and weed crumbs littering the lining of his bag. He scoops up a handful, replete with broken pencil leads, bits of granola, and a crumpled index card with 64 tiny pictures of Scooby-Doo on it and thrusts it on Derek.

"Dude, what the fuck?" Derek hops backwards, a disgusted look on his face. "Don't fucking touch me with that acid. I'm not trying to trip balls this morning. Fuck's sake, man. Wrap that shit up in some tin foil or something."

Lyle's mind goes blank. Imagine a skydiver. He is falling precipitously from an airplane, the ground steadily rushing up to him, when he pulls his parachute cord and nothing happens. He might shit himself in midair, scream "wait! wait!" at the ground, cry for his mommy, assume the position of a frightened cat, arms and feet out, back arched, in a vain attempt to keep the earth from smacking him in the face. Then imagine him crashing through a greenhouse, the entire building shattering explosively, shards of glass continuing to rain down on the splatter pattern that was his body. Then compress this entire sequence into a single point in time creating a singularity of panic, horror and hideous violence. This is how Lyle feels.

The electrical storm raging in Lyle's brain, combined with several dozen acid trips worth of serotonin and dopamine, and gobs of adrenaline and norepinephrine and other primal fight-or-flight hormones, leave Lyle utterly catatonic. His stash drops to the ground as if his cupped hands were a sieve. His jaw quivers.

"Well shit. Don't just drop it on the ground. Lyle? Lyle?"

The words echo in his head as if they are coming from a great distance. He steps back, but trips on an uneven floorboard and falls backwards through the bathroom door. His head smacks against the wall in the hallway. Defeated and bewildered, he stares into the bathroom. Steam swirls and rises like dry ice. Derek, wrapped in a towel, steps over Lyle. He is not in a hurry, and he does not look back. In his absence, the only sound left to fill the void of Lyle's mind is the bathroom fan. It pulls curls of steam up towards its hidden blades only to expel them out of the house and into oblivion. The mechanical drone howls like wind past the ears of a man falling from great heights. He lies limp against the wall and lets his mind rise with the steam.

Big Trouble

You can hear Tito coming down the hall.

The bell rings and he's not there and the teachers are always looking like "maybe he's not coming" or "maybe they finally bounced him" but sure enough a couple minutes into class someone's iced coffee starts rippling like it's *Jurassic Park* and here comes Tito. Most of the time he just comes in and finds his seat and it's not like he's even trying to be disruptive, but like, the guy is just loud. Or maybe the world around him just gets quiet as he passes through, like he's some kind of energy vacuum, absorbing all the noise and electricity within a five foot radius and he's just supercharged and buzzing like a pylon. For real, though: this kid can not sit still to save his life. This kid, everyday, is itchy as all hell. Not like he's scratching himself, but shit, it's like he's on a treadmill set just a little too fast and if he ever stops moving it will spit him off and leave him flailing forever.

Tito can make an entrance when he wants to. He'll slap some shit right off a kid's desk. Or he'll swipe someone's phone and dangle it in front of them. Or he'll remember he forgot something and he'll start walking around asking to borrow a pencil or a piece of paper or a swig of someone's Red Bull or something while the teacher's trying to say some shit. And then the teacher will try to get a hold on it but Tito will have something smart to say. He's got some kind of excuse, or he just really needs this one thing, or he's just playing, or he just really actually forgot all of his stuff and how is he supposed to do any fucking work without any of his fucking stuff.

Every once in a while, though, he'll really put on a show. He'll come in with a grin and he'll look at whoever's sitting next to him like "watch this shit" and you just know he's about to curbstomp this crusty old teacher's day. He'll shout out "Hey teach, it smells like my asshole in here." Or "Hey teach, you gay? You tryna get gay, teach?" Or "Hey teach, I heard you in the shitter earlier. Goddamn, bro. What you eatin, teach?" And the teacher will either give him this disapproving, cooing, drawn out "Tiiiitooo" or a sharp "Tito!" Or a blustery "Get out of my classroom!" Or an exhausted, droopy "Go to the office, Tito." It depends on the teacher. And the time of year. But by springtime even the cool teachers have had it up to here with him.

Even on Tito's most chill days he won't make it past ten minutes before he's gotta go to the bathroom or get a drink or get something from his locker. The teachers either let him go because they can't deal with him in that moment, or they'll tell him no, so he'll wait for them to turn around and then slip out of there like a goddamn fresh-caught fish. You wouldn't believe it, man. Like a goddamn cat. Even the other kids won't see him slip out, it's just suddenly like, where's Tito? But then everyone gets back to whatever they're doing because now he's some- one else's problem. He's out there wandering the halls, vaping

Juuls in the bathroom, sending dumbass snaps, dapping up the custodians. At lunch he'll go up to whichever teachers are on lunch duty and dap them up and try to get a laugh out of them, talk about basketball or whatever, even if he just fucked up their morning classes. And it's like it's all good. They probably know that Tito's not a bad dude. He's just always in trouble. So they always forgive him. And maybe that's the closest thing to love Tito's got.

It's not even his fault at this point, to be honest. At least not all the time. Other kids be trolling him daily. Like they'll be screwing around in class making fart noises or whatever and then say "Tito, stop!" Or "Tito, quit it already," even though Tito ain't doing nothing, but the teacher will turn around and holler at Tito and he'll say he wasn't doing nothing while the trolls are snickering and hiding their grins. No one believes him anymore, though, so he'll just get sent packing for doing nothing. Sometimes they'll just make him sit in the front office. Literally just sit there, not even making him do work. And it's sad as fuck when you walk past the office and you see him just sitting at a table by himself staring at the wall, bouncing his leg, looking uncomfortable and confused.

He does get in fights, though. Most of the time he just plays too rough. The problem is that he's kinda big, bigger than most, and he's scarier than he realizes. It's usually on the basketball court. Someone will get heated and it will end with Tito shoving someone or putting someone in a choke hold. Sometimes he throws hands, but it never goes to the ground. This one time, though, he almost broke Benny Crowder's neck in middle school. Usual deal, just playing ball, then next thing you know

Tito's wrangling this kid like an ornery calf on branding day until he passes out. The teachers on lunch duty got all excited and started screaming at Tito big time, screaming at him while he's sitting on the ground crying so hard he's got snots coming out of his nose.

It's not just roughhousing with him, though. He can get angry – red in the face, foaming at the mouth angry. The thing is kids give him a lot of shit. Every now and then some nutsack will want to rattle his chains and get up in his face and call him a retard. That'll get Tito throwing hands fast. And fair enough, you can't be calling people retarded no more, especially when they're actually... well, you know. Maybe Tito's not retarded, but he can't really read. He's been in those special ed classes since at least 3rd grade. He'd always be getting called out of class by some smiley sped tutor or working with one of those crusty teacher aides. It was always this fat fucking elephant that followed Tito from class to class and grade to grade.

Now he's in the reading class with the, like, five other Mexican kids in school, but he doesn't speak Spanish, and they're all like "you don't speak English *or* Spanish? The fuck?" And then they clown on him in Spanish and poor Tito knows it but he wants to be friends with them anyway so he just goes full jester because maybe being laughed at isn't that different from making people laugh? So one day he swipes his mom's hash oil vape pen off the couch and starts getting baked AF all day long, toking on his walk to school, blowing clouds in the hallway when no one's looking, getting straight ripped in the boy's bathroom, hot-boxing the shit out of Mason Graham's Jeep with a bunch of other playboys and sack-tappers before floating into the lunchroom and scarfing down some cafeteria pizza and Red Bulls. Then he walks around with his eyes as red as donkey dongs, grinning like a goddamn fool, getting mad giggles from everyone.

He got away with it for a while. He was a little more mellow and would sleep through his last few classes and his teachers weren't about to complain about it. But the office eventually got wind of it, so one day Principle Driscoll shows up to sixth period with a walkie-talkie and pulls him out of class and searches his shit, and obviously he's got grass and hash vapes and all that in his locker because obviously Mason Graham asked him to hold it for him and obviously Tito said fuck yeah, I got your back, bro. So Tito gets the ole OSS because he's already had like seven in-school suspensions this year and the ISS lady has had it up to here with him. They call his mom in for a meeting because he's in big trouble now, and she doesn't pick up at first, but eventually they get ahold of her and she says she'll be there soon, but next thing you know it's five o'clock and everyone's gone and his mom's not picking up the phone anymore, so Ms. Driscoll finally gives up and lets Tito walk home.

The next morning he wakes up and his mom is all like why the fuck are you still here? So he tells her and she does this whole what-the-fuck-is-wrong-with-you thing and some why-can't-you-just-behave bit and that she has had it absolutely up to fucking here with him. Then she says she has to go to work and she does. So now it's just Tito and Shithead Steve, his mom's creepy-ass boyfriend, the one who got rolled trying to cook meth in the trailer park a few years ago. He's got a joint in his mouth and his hand down his boxers and everything smells like burned plastic and rotten beer so Tito dips and just starts walking. He figures Gannon might be ditching and heads to his house. Well, where he lives anyway.

Straight up: Cade Gannon is fucking scary. He lives in an old camper on his, like, ex-stepdad's lot just east of town. He's got this jet black hair that he parts down the middle and pushes behind his ears, and these gold-rimmed bottle cap sunglasses, and this butterfly knife that he likes flashing and flipping just to make everyone wonder if maybe he is actually legit psychotic. So Tito shows up at Cade's camper and they rip bongs and watch porn on Cade's phone and get drunk and go into the woods and shoot empty beer cans with airsoft guns. Then they're back at the camper sucking down a blunt and Cade asks Tito if he'd like to make some money. Tito says fuck yeah, bro, I'm tryna buy my own car so I can move out ASAP, tryna make some serious coin so I can get my own place and not have to worry about shit no more. So Cade, flipping his butterfly knife like he's not even thinking about it, tells Tito that he's tryna move some drugs, but the heat is too hot and all the kids at school be snitching on him. He tells Tito that he can keep 25% of the cut if he can unload this entire box of hash oil vape cartridges which Cade says he found and not to fucking worry about it. Tito says he's not sure, that he's in pretty big trouble as is, and Cade asks him if he's a pussy. And then he leaps out his chair and puts the butterfly knife up to Tito's neck and asks him if he's a fucking pussy-ass bitch. Then he starts laughing and taps Tito on the cheek and says he's just fucking around, but for real though, people will think you're hard as fuck if you're pushing drugs. Everyone will think you're a serious fucking G and no one will mess with you no more. And all the girls will think you're way sexy and you'll get invited to all the parties and you'll be fucking loaded, getting high whenever you want, buying whatever you want.

And it's true. Nobody disrespects Cade. Cade's always got a wad of cash and has sweet airsoft guns and fancy bongs and Red Bulls on Red Bulls. Tito looks up and away but all he sees is himself wearing bling and packing heat and getting lap dances from girls with big tits and high heels. Fuck yeah, son, he says. Fuck *yes*, son. And he's so excited he gets up and starts pacing up and down the camper saying fuck yes, son, and tells Cade that he won't let him down. He asks if he should come back and get a few cartridges at a time but Cade says nah, son you gotta take the whole load now and don't fucking tell anyone where you got it. He stops flipping his knife and points it at Tito and says, just remember, if I don't get every goddamn penny, I'm going to cut your fucking dick off.

So Tito scoops all the hash cartridges into the pouch in his hoodie and walks home in the rain with his chest out because now he's a pusha man and soon he'll be able to buy real air pods and fresh Jordans and maybe he'll even start rapping and drop a mixtape and next thing you know he'll be flashing middle fingers while he roars onto the interstate in his brand new Maserati, never to return.

For the rest of the week he gets high on his own supply and hangs around the park and the Dairy Queen and the trailer park trying to unload some hash, but it's slow going. On Monday he's allowed back to school and he sells five cartridges in gym class alone. At lunch he sells a bunch to Mason Graham and his friends and they get totally blitzed in his Jeep and one of them says he should advertise, let people know he's open for business. By now Tito's got a fat stack of cash and he is straight feeling himself, so he takes a few selfies blowing vape clouds, fanning himself with dollar bills, holding a handful of little vape cartridges, and sends them out on SnapChat with the caption HMU in the boys bthroom, 20$ a pop.

So he ditches fifth period and hangs out in the boys bathroom. It smells like gnarly after-lunch Red Bull dumps and hash smoke and he sells a few cartridges and scares a few Freshmen, but after about 30 minutes Principal Driscoll shows up with her walkie-talkie and Vice Principal Gardner is there too, also with a walkie-talkie, because Tito forgot that not everyone who follows him on SnapChat is chill, and some cheese-eater obviously took screenshots of his snaps and narced on him. They have this stupid back and forth where Tito insists that he's just got mad diarrhea and they don't have the right to search his shit and they need a warrant and they're just picking on him because he's brown, but they haul his ass into the office and make him sit there alone at the conference table until the sheriff shows up and finds the wad of cash and handful of hash cartridges in his hoodie pouch. Then the sheriff puts him in handcuffs and Tito starts crying because he's never been in handcuffs before and he's high out of his goddamn gourd and he knows he's in big trouble now. The sheriff tells the principal that these cartridges match the ones that were stolen from a dispensary in Eugene and then he looks down at Tito who can't look up at him and says, son, you're 17. Do you know what that means, son? They call his mom and she says she'll be there soon.

The grownups step out of the office but Tito can hear them talking about him, saying that the good people of this community have completely had it up to here with him. Saying Tito just keeps making bad choices, has always been making bad choices, and that it's tough and it's sad but if they just keep forgiving him he'll never learn his lesson. Then everything starts moving faster and faster and Tito can feel the whole world rushing away from him. He starts saying things like wait and please over and over again, and he feels almost like he's falling up, floating away, flailing for something to hold onto. He's howling please, please through tears and hiccups, begging for someone, anyone, to wrap him up, pin him to the ground, and smother him.

Intake Report

Juneau Batterer Intervention Program

Date of Intake: 1.16.2017

Interviewer: Ian Christensen

Location of Interview: Lemon Creek Corrections Center

Participant Information:

Name: Cody Ward
DOB: 2.20.1970

Referral Origin: Juneau District Attorney

Referral Case Number: 1JU–6472–01

Referral Charges: Aggravated assault in the first degree

Victim: Erica Swale

Contact with Victim: No

Personal History:

Cody Ward was born on February 20th, 1970 in Juneau, Alaska. At the time, his father worked at a gold mine on Chichagof Island and was consequently absent for most of Mr. Ward's early childhood. Mr. Ward noted that his father was white and his mother was Native Alaskan. He further stated that his father was "much older" than his mother. Mr. Ward was unable to recall significant details about his early childhood in Juneau, aside from the birth of his younger brother, Sebastian, when he was four years old.

Around this time, Mr. Ward's father quit working at the mine and moved the family to a remote homestead on the southern side of Chichagof Island. Upon relocating to the homestead, Mr. Ward, his mother, and his brother would not leave for nearly five years. However, Mr. Ward's father would regularly travel to town for weeks on end, ostensibly on supply runs.

According to Mr. Ward, the homestead consisted of a main cabin and several outbuildings constructed on a narrow, rocky shoreline that ran up against dense rainforest. The cabin was furnished when they arrived, but was in a state weatherbeaten disrepair. Mr. Ward speculated that his father won the property in a poker game at the mining camp; however, he also noted that his father refused to ever discuss the origins or history of the property. There was no electricity or plumbing. The cabin was heated by a wood stove and water was fetched from a nearby creek. Mr. Ward noted that his father maintained strict control over the firewood, lamp oil, and the diesel generator. The family subsisted largely on wild-caught fish supplemented by bulk supplies of rice and canned goods purchased in town.

Mr. Ward recalled that his father spent a great deal of time out at sea fishing, maintaining his boat, or working in the woodshop. However, during inclement weather they would be confined to the cabin for extended periods of time. He noted that during the winter months he and his brother would huddle under blankets in the main room while his father "did things" to his mother in the bedroom. Mr. Ward recalled watching his father hone his various knives and blades and clean his rifles at the table on a near daily basis.

Mr. Ward described his younger brother, Sebastian, as autistic and non-verbal. He "would go blank" in the presence of their father, but in his absence, Sebastian was liable to explode into "screaming fits" that reportedly lasted for "hours and days." Mr. Ward remembered seeing his mother sobbing as she tried and failed to soothe Sebastian. Mr. Ward stated that his mother eventually took to "chaining" Sebastian to the "bunkhouse." When asked for clarification on the bunkhouse, Mr. Ward stated that it was a small out-building that contained "a rusty metal bed" and a "rotten mattress." When asked if his father built the bunkhouse, Mr. Ward stated that the bunk house had been there when they arrived. When asked if his use of the word "chained" was literal, he stated that he meant that there were literal chains in the bunkhouse. When asked if the chains were also in the bunkhouse when they arrived, Mr. Ward stated that he believed so.

Mr. Ward reported witnessing his father violently assault his mother on multiple occasions. He recalled seeing his father grab his mother by the hair and "throw her around the room." He recalled an incident when he was eight years old in which he had to treat his mother's broken facial bones after an assault and how she had to "relearn how to talk" as the result of a suspected traumatic brain injury. Mr. Ward indicated that his mother became erratic following that particular incident and began making attempts to escape. This resulted in Mr. Ward's father locking all of their shoes in a chest. Mr. Ward recalled his father keeping the key to the chest on a ring of keys on his belt.

Mr. Ward noted that his mother's mental state deteriorated rapidly. She struggled to speak and would "scream and cry and pull her hair" in frustration. Mr. Ward recalled that one night his mother "pulled a knife" on his father. Based on Mr. Ward's account, his mother walked up behind his father while he was repairing a boat engine and attempted to stab him in the neck with a screwdriver. However, Mr. Ward's father overpowered her before she was able to injure him. Mr. Ward stated that his father then beat her unconscious and dragged her by the hair to the bunkhouse. Mr. Ward became responsible for delivering food and water to his mother. His father would send him out with dinner scraps and a bucket of water, which he would replace with the previous bucket that his mother was forced to use as a latrine. His mother would try to talk to him and hold him, but he stated that "she scared him." He recalled seeing her huddled in the corner wrapped in a thin blanket, her ankle chained to the wall. She had pulled out chunks of her hair and had bloody scars on her wrists and all over her body from where she cut herself on the exposed mattress springs. Mr. Ward clarified that these were self-inflicted wounds. Mr. Ward further noted that Sebastian's behavior became unmanageable, and his father had taken to beating him unconscious or sedating him with alcohol to make him stop screaming. Eventually, his father brought Sebastian out to the bunkhouse and chained him up with his mother.

Mr. Ward stated that after some time, his father finished fixing the boat engine and left the homestead. Mr. Ward recalled not freeing his mother or brother out of fear that his father would return at a moment's notice. His father, however, had left them without any food and had taken the keys to everything with him. After about a week, he began to believe that his father had left them for dead. He broke into his father's tool shed and freed his mother and brother with a large file. Mr. Ward recalled his mother embracing him and crying and apologizing to him. According to Mr. Ward, she repeated, stuttering, "I'm sorry, I'm so sorry," as she ran her fingers through his hair. He further recalled pulling away from his mother and running back to the house. From the window, he saw her emerge from the toolshed holding a small axe. He watched her limp back to the bunkhouse, weighed down by the ankle cuff and a few feet of chain. He ran barefoot back across the shore to "save his brother" but found his mother "hacking [Sebastian] to pieces." Mr. Ward stated that there was so much blood that it even got on him as he stood frozen in the doorway. See transcription below.

WARD:

> She didn't stop until the axe was hitting the floor and getting stuck in the boards. She started crying and kept saying she was sorry over and over again. I went to go put my hand on her shoulder or something, I don't know, but she grabbed my wrist and threw me onto the floor. I tried to get up, but it was too slippery, so I rolled under the bed before she could pull the axe from the boards. She started hacking away at the bed, and I could see the axe ripping

through the mattress and clanging on the frame. She tired herself out, and I bolted right past her into the forest. I kept hearing her calling my name like a lost dog, saying she was sorry and asking me to come back. But she went dead silent the second the old man's boat came grumbling up the channel. I hid in the brush and listened to the whole thing. Listened to her scream. Then him scream. And then the gunshot. And then it was finally quiet.

Mr. Ward stated that he stayed hidden in the forest for the rest of the day and the following night. He returned to the homestead to find his father delirious with fever, a bloody, stinking rag wrapped around his partially severed foot. Mr. Ward recalled ignoring his father's demands for water and help. Mr. Ward stated that he "watched him die."

When asked how he reflected on this experience now as an adult, Mr. Ward stated that he did not think about it.

Mr. Ward further recalled that he remained at the homestead for an unknown number of days or possibly weeks following the murders. He stated that he had no memory of this time period or of piloting the boat into the sound.

An article published in the Juneau Empire on August 8th, 1979 ran the headline "Miners Rescue Orphan Found Adrift in Hoonah Sound." According to the article, a boat ferrying mine workers to a camp on Chichagof Island spotted a damaged vessel (described as a small schooner) east of Ushk Bay and investigated. They discovered Mr. Ward "emaciated and unresponsive" on board and brought him to Angoon. Alaska State Troopers relocated Mr. Ward to Juneau and placed him in the care of the

Office of Children's Services. According to the article, Alaska State Troopers opened an investigation into the case. Documents requested from the AST archives revealed that attempts to locate the homestead were unsuccessful. Mr. Ward was unable to give authorities any meaningful directions or descriptions of the homestead, and the investigation concluded after an unsuccessful reconnaissance search of the Hoonah Sound.

Mr. Ward's OCS case file stated that he was assigned to a group home in Juneau and that attempts to locate any living family were unsuccessful. OCS found Mr. Ward's birth certificate via hospital records from 2.20.1970 revealing that Mr. Ward is the son of Jeremiah Ward (b. 1930) and Evelyn Ward (b. 1952). This indicates that Mr. Ward's mother was 17-18 years old at the time of his birth. Mr. Ward's case manager was unable to find a marriage certificate for his parents, and his mother's maiden name was never learned.

According to OCS records, Mr. Ward spoke "only in a low whisper" and did not meaningfully interact with other children at the group home. The report indicates that Mr. Ward was completely illiterate and had minimal mathematical competencies. Mr. Ward was enrolled in intensive educational remediation through OCS. However, four months into his stay, Mr. Ward assaulted a staff member of the group home, evidently biting the staff member's thumb so severely that he required hospitalization. A psychiatrist diagnosed Mr. Ward with antisocial personality disorder and acute psychosis. When asked about the assault, Mr. Ward stated that the staff member screamed at him and berated him and he "just wanted him to stop screaming." Mr. Ward was transferred to Juneau Juvenile

Correctional Center and began a course of psychotropic medication. Mr. Ward stated that he has little memory of this period of his life.

When he was 15, Mr. Ward was deemed well enough for foster care and was transferred to a home in Auk Bay. Shortly after his arrival, another foster child in the home reported to OCS that Mr. Ward had sodomized a pet cat with a ballpoint pen. OCS was unable to corroborate the accusation and Mr. Ward was allowed to continue living in the home. Two years later, a foster sibling reported to OCS that Mr. Ward had molested her. OCS could not corroborate the accusation and the matter was not investigated further. During the interview, Mr. Ward denied the allegations and stated that the foster sibling in question was a compulsive liar.

Mr. Ward did not complete high school and moved out of foster care immediately upon turning 18. The boat on which Mr. Ward was rescued still technically belonged to him, and he reclaimed it from the State of Alaska on his 18th birthday. According to OCS, Mr. Ward lived in his boat and began work at a salmon cannery in Juneau. Mr. Ward was exited from OCS care on 2.20.1988.

Criminal History:

10.20.1991

- JPD responded to an altercation at The Viking in downtown Juneau. Officers arrived at the scene at 12:37 AM. Witnesses stated that Mr. Ward had been inappropriately touching women in the bar. An altercation with bouncers ensued and Mr. Ward was ejected from the bar. The bartender notified police, but Mr. Ward was no longer at the scene upon arrival. Police tracked down Mr. Ward at his residence the next morning and cited him for drunk and disorderly conduct. Mr. Ward was sentenced to 40 hours of community service.

- Mr. Ward stated that he had no memory of the night at the bar and that he completed the community service without incident.

4.8.1992

- JPD responded to a domestic violence complaint at Mr. Ward's residence. A passerby notified police of "a woman screaming for help" in the Juneau-Douglas Harbor. Officers arrived at the scene and separated Mr. Ward and one Julia Flores. The police report noted that officers knew Ms. Flores from prior contacts and that she had previously been charged with solicitation. Ms. Flores stated that Mr. Ward had not allowed her to leave the boat by blocking her exit with his body and physically restraining her. Mr. Ward stated that Ms. Flores had just "gone crazy" and that he was trying to calm her down. Officers ensured that Ms. Flores left the premises and no arrests were made.

- Mr. Ward stated that he stands by his statements in the police report. Mr. Ward described Ms. Flores as "a lying whore," and stated that they had an "on-again off-again" relationship for approximately two years.

1.9.1994

- JPD detectives questioned Mr. Ward in the disappearance of his co-worker, Maria Clark. Ms. Clark did not return from work at the cannery on the night of 1.5.1994. According to the case file, Ms. Clark had filed a complaint with HR regarding Mr. Ward's behavior three weeks prior to her disappearance. The complaint alleged that Mr. Ward would frequently stare at her for extended periods of time. She requested to be moved to another section on the assembly line, but evidently her complaint and request went ignored. Detectives questioned Mr. Ward at work, but he stated that he was unaware of any complaints made against him and further stated that he had never met Ms. Clark. On the night of her disappearance, Mr. Ward had worked overtime cleaning the assembly line. This alibi checked out, and Mr. Ward was not listed as a suspect in the case. Ms. Clark was never found and the case remains open.
- Mr. Ward stated that he never had any contact with Ms. Clark. When asked why he chose to leave his job at the cannery two weeks later, Mr. Ward stated that he got a job on a crab boat up north and had been eager to leave Juneau for some time.

9.29.2004

- An AST marine patrol unit intercepted Mr. Ward north of Angoon. A trooper had observed through binoculars what appeared to be "significant quantities of blood" on the deck of Mr. Ward's boat. Two troopers boarded Mr. Ward's boat with Mr. Ward's consent. Mr. Ward showed the troopers a large chest full of venison stowed on deck. Mr. Ward stated that he had butchered the deer on his boat in an effort to avoid contact with bears and then thrown the carcass overboard. Troopers did not conduct a search of the boat. AST cited Mr. Ward for poaching and he was fined $5,000 dollars and was not allowed to obtain hunting tags for three years. Mr. Ward did not pay the penalty and the fee remains outstanding.

- Mr. Ward stated that he lived primarily on his boat in between fishing seasons and would dock in various communities throughout the Inside Passage for extended periods of time. Mr. Ward noted that when the weather was favorable, he would anchor in the backcountry and subsist on fishing and hunting. When asked why he had not paid his fine he said "because they can go fuck themselves."

Referral Incident:

Mr. Ward stated that in 2014 he began a relationship with Erica Swale. Ms. Swale worked as a waitress at the Misty Bay Lodge in Hoonah where Mr. Ward would often eat while he was in town. One day, Mr. Ward invited her to go out on his boat and she agreed. Mr. Ward stated that they were "into simi-lar things." Mr. Ward noted that they would "hook up" when he was in town and their relationship was strictly sexual.

According to the arrest report, on November 20th 2016, Mr. Ward and Ms. Swale were seen leaving the Misty Bay Lodge together at approximately 4:30 PM. Approximately twenty min-utes later, a passerby walked into the Hoonah Public Safety office and reported that she had heard "shouting and crying" coming from a small schooner in the marina. The police officer on duty walked to the harbor to investigate and saw "a large man carrying what appeared to be an unconscious woman into the galley of the boat." Before the officer was able to intervene, the schooner in question departed into the channel. The officer contacted AST marine patrol who dispatched a patrol boat from Gustavus. Mr. Ward's schooner was intercepted approximately one hour later northeast of Hoonah. Mr. Ward told troopers that there was no one onboard the boat, but troopers believed that they had probable cause to search the vessel. Troopers located a semi-conscious Ms. Swale "hogtied and gagged" in the galley of the schooner. Troopers requested a helicopter medical evacuation for Ms. Swale and she was transported to Juneau for treatment. Arrest reports indicate that Ms. Swale suffered a broken orbital bone, a broken nose, a severe concussion, blunt force trauma to the occipital lobe of her skull, and three broken ribs. Mr. Ward was placed under arrest and transported to Juneau for processing.

The arrest report included a transcript from an interview with Ms. Swale three days after the incident. Ms. Swale stated that she and Mr. Ward had a casual relationship for over a year.

Ms. Swale revealed that their relationship was based on a mutual interest in BDSM. On the night of the incident, Ms. Swale willingly boarded Mr. Ward's schooner, but once on board Mr. Ward began undocking from the marina. Ms. Swale told Mr. Ward that she did not want to leave the marina, but Mr. Ward insisted that they sail to a secluded location. Ms. Swale stated that she attempted to get off the boat, but Mr. Ward "grabbed [her] by the hair" and "threw [her] to the ground." Ms. Swale began "crying for help" but Mr. Ward "knocked [her] out cold." Ms. Swale recalled coming to in the galley of the boat and realizing that they were well into the channel. She feared that Mr. Ward would kill her, so she went back on deck and attempted to jump off the boat. Ms. Swale recalled that it was "dark and raining and cold" but suspected it was her last chance to escape. When asked if she had any idea where Mr. Ward was taking her, Ms. Swale stated that Mr. Ward had previously mentioned on multiple occasions that he had "a homestead on the other side of the island," and that he wanted to take her there "for vacation" sometime. However, Mr. Ward saw her when she emerged on deck. Ms. Swale said she hesitated while climbing the rail and Mr. Ward restrained her so tightly that she "heard [her] ribs crack." Mr. Ward then carried her back down to the galley where he gagged her with a BDSM ball gag and hogtied her.

During police interrogation, Mr. Ward stated that he and Ms. Swale had gone to his boat to have sex. He further stated that Ms. Swale lost her footing on the boat and fell and hit her head. Mr. Ward asserted that Ms. Swale quickly regained consciousness but was "acting crazy." He believed that she needed medical attention, so he attempted to make the approximately 3 hour boat trip to Juneau to get her to the hospital. However, at some point during the trip, Ms. Swale "lost her mind" and attempted to "kill herself" by jumping off the boat. Mr. Ward was ultimately charged with Attempted Kidnapping and 1st Degree Aggravated Assault, but the charge of Attempted Kidnapping was dropped as a part of a plea deal. Mr. Ward was sentenced to 14 months in prison and completion of the Juneau Batterer Intervention Program.

When pressed on the extent of her injuries, Mr. Ward insisted that Ms. Swale's broken facial bones and concussion were a result of her losing her balance and falling. The interviewer noted that it seemed impossible that she could injure both her face and the back of her head in a single fall. Mr. Ward became defensive and stated "that's what happened." In regard to Ms. Swale's broken ribs, Mr. Ward stated again that Ms. Swale was trying to kill herself and he needed to give her "a bear hug" to keep her on board. The interviewer noted that to break three ribs requires tremendous pressure, well beyond what was necessary to restrain someone. Then Mr. Ward said "I just wanted her to stop screaming." Mr. Ward became agitated and repeated with increasing volume and intensity "I just wanted her to stop screaming." The interviewer interrupted Mr. Ward and asked him to calm down. At this point, the interviewer noted how Mr. Ward's posture wilted and he stared unflinchingly at the table. What followed is transcribed below:

INT: Cody, can you hear me?
(Silence)
INT: Cody?

(Silence)

WARD: (In a low whisper) I just wanted her to stop screaming.

INT:Who did you want to stop screaming?

(Silence)

INT:Cody, who did you want to stop screaming?

(Silence)

WARD: (Whispered) My mommy.

INT:You wanted your mother to stop screaming?

WARD:I had to make her stop screaming.

INT:How did you make your mother stop screaming?

WARD:I hit her.

INT: You hit your mother with your hands?

WARD: With the axe.

(Silence)

INT:You hit your mother with an axe?

(Silence)

INT:Did you hit anyone else with an axe?

(Silence)

INT: Who else did you hit with the axe?

WARD:Sebastian.

(Silence)

WARD: And my daddy.

(Silence)

INT: What happened after you hit them with the axe?

WARD:They stopped screaming.

(Silence)

INT:Where were you and Erica going?

(Silence)

INT:Cody, where were you taking Erica?

(Silence)

WARD: I just wanted her to stop screaming.

INT:Cody, where were you taking Erica?

WARD:(Shouting) I just wanted her to stop screaming. I just wanted her to stop screaming.

Mr. Ward became increasingly agitated and continued shouting "I just wanted her to stop screaming" as he banged on the table with his fists. The prison guard on duty came into the interview room upon hearing the commotion. Mr. Ward suddenly became quiet and lifted his gaze. The interviewer noted that Mr. Ward stared bewilderedly at the ring of keys still in the guard's hand. The guard escorted Mr. Ward back to the cell block without incident.

Intake Assessment:

JBIP staff evaluate Mr. Ward as having an extremely high risk of lethality. The details of the referral incident alone are sufficient to support this analysis, but the evidence collected herein suggests that the scope and scale of Mr. Ward's abuse and violence against women is potentially vast. The extent of Mr. Ward's childhood trauma is profound, and the apparent dissociative episode indicates that said trauma has thoroughly injured his psychology in potentially dangerous ways. JBIP staff strongly recommend that Mr. Ward receive comprehensive mental health services while incarcerated.

JBIP staff further recommend that every effort be made to investigate the disappearance of Mr. Ward's family. The homestead in question is potentially the scene of numerous crimes spanning decades. JBIP staff has forwarded copies of this intake assessment to AWARE and the Alaska chapter of Missing and Murdered Indigenous Women and requested help in cross-referencing missing person's reports in Southeast Alaska with Mr. Ward's whereabouts. Additionally, JBIP staff strongly recommend that the District Attorney's office re-examine the disappearance of Maria Clark and investigate Mr. Ward as a person of interest.

JBIP staff recommends that Mr. Ward be enrolled in JBIP's full 52-week course.

Eden Prime

Our colony was once a paradise.

We began in Earth Year 2235 when our Earth Parents landed some 400 kilometers south of the Martian north pole. All 15 of them survived the voyage and established Eden Prime over the course of three Earth years. To survive the radiation, have a constant source of water, live under atmospheric pressure comparable to Earth, and harness geothermal energy, they built our colony 140 meters below the surface of Mars. The Earth Parents lived in the space ship while they mined down to safe depths and built the vast antechamber where we congregated for ceremony and discourse. They also constructed the medical chamber, the sustenance chamber, the printing chamber, and the control chamber with the aid of the many machines that accompanied them from Earth. They converted Martian soil into a liquid polymer, thus creating an infinitely malleable and nearly indestructible building material. Every tunnel, every chamber, every bed, every utensil was the same rusty red of Mars herself. The Martian soil could be converted into many other substances; fibers, paper, ink, machine oil. Mars gave us many gifts.

The Alpha Cohort was born in EY 2240. All eight Earth Mothers gave birth to one child. The Beta Cohort was born 1.5 EY later. All told, the Earth Mothers bore five cohorts. The Earth Parents schooled these initial cohorts in how to operate the colony and avoid the follies of our Earthling ancestors. This knowledge was collected in the *Charter of Eden Prime,* now known verbatim in the heart of every initiated colonist.

The Charter stipulated that eight new colonists were to be born every year. Genetic assays were done, and five breeding pairs were selected to maximize genetic diversity. 10 EY after our birth, we entered initiation, where we were sterilized and given neural implants that erased the many urges which corrupted our ancestors. However, if selected for copulation in adulthood, the sterilization was reversed and the implant deactivated until reproduction was successful. Offspring never learned which of their elders birthed them, and breeders never knew their progeny. The Charter stated that familial allegiance divided and corrupted our ancestors. On Eden Prime, we were all one family.

For our first 10 EY, we were raised by caregivers and taught foundational knowledge. After initiation we relocated to our living chamber, where we lived together as a cohort for the next 55 EY until we were retired into the soil from which our sustenance grew. Also upon initiation we were assigned to our vocations, thus commencing our apprenticeships. Our elders schooled us in the unique skills of our respective vocations, as well as in the history of our ancestors. Every vocation was as important as the rest. Some of us were tunnelers, or farmers, or custodians, or printers, or sustenance preparers. There were also caregivers, water managers, oxygen managers, geothermal engineers, electrical engineers, and Charter keepers. Some jobs, such as tunneling, required many colonists. Some, like mine, required only two. The Charter warned of special rewards for our labor. Our ancestors once traded their labor for something called capital and then traded that capital for personal possessions. The Charter states that this led to the destruction of Earth. On Eden Prime, we had no personal possessions, and our labor was our greatest pride.

Our communication with Earth was limited to our annual transaction. Our colony sprouted amid a large selenium deposit and we excavated selenium as a byproduct of our expansion. We then packaged it in great metal crates and sent it to the surface through an airlocked elevator shaft at the beginning of every new Earth Year. A colossal vessel descended into the Martian atmosphere, raising the selenium with powerful magnets. In exchange, these same ships returned the metal crates with materials Mars could not provide for us, such as our implants, essential machinery, minerals and chemicals, computer chips and circuit boards, the red lights that lit our tunnels and chambers, and the white lights that grew our sustenance. This was the extent of our communication. The Earth Parents warned us of corruption by the Earthlings. Direct contact with Earthlings was only possible during brief moments of orbital intersection, and the Charter limited such communication to requests for specific materials. We knew nothing of other colonies, save for their existence hundreds, if not thousands of miles away.

None of us had ever touched the surface. It could be viewed only through a single periscope in the control room. There was only desert and the defunct machines and structures of the Earth Parents' initial settlement. There was nothing for us there. Everything we needed was in our colony. We had each other. We congregated before and after every work shift in the dining chamber for sustenance consumption. Each colonist was assigned a seat, and that seat rotated every meal so that every colonist personally interacted with every other colonist. We knew each other, we were fond of each other, we cared for each other. We had community meetings every .1 EY in the ante-chamber. We gave thanks to our Earth Parents, remembered their sacrifices, discussed sections of the Charter, and shared updates from our different vocational domains.

We lived in peace and harmony and happiness for many generations. Our colony expanded out by many kilometers and reached depths of 400 meters. We achieved our stable maximum population of 520. We had fulfilled the Earth Parents' greatest dreams.

But now we live in darkness.

Sometime ago — I cannot honestly say how long — an electro-magnetic surge precipitated a catastrophic colony-wide power failure. Eden Prime was instantly plunged into darkness. We convened in the antechamber, guided through the darkness by only our memories. We awaited news from the various vocational domains. The geothermal engineers suspected that some unforeseeable electromagnetic phenomenon occurred in the planet's core and short circuited the entirety of the colony's electrical system. The engineers stated that the geothermal generator was completely destroyed and would require machinery from Earth to repair. The elder communication engineer confirmed that without power, there was no way to send a message to Earth. The elder astronomer confirmed that the next scheduled selenium retrieval was not for another .91 Earth Years. A hush fell over us as the prospect of protracted, complete darkness sank in. We would have to wait for Earthlings to see that no selenium was recovered, attempt to communicate with us, and then finally send a reconnaissance team to assist us. The senior astronomer estimated it could be over 1.5 EY before rescue.

A great murmuring arose in the antechamber. The elder sustenance grower declared that there was enough reserve sustenance to feed the entire colony for 1 EY if austerity rations were implemented. Without any electricity for light, though, it would be impossible to grow new food. The elder water manager spoke up, stating that the water reserves would last about as long. The elder oxygen manager estimated that we could have two years of oxygen if segments of the colony were sealed, and the ventilation system could theoretically be powered by manually cranking the ventilators. A geothermal engineer stated that the geothermal vents would keep the colony at a survivable temperature indefinitely. One of us spoke up to ask who would calculate these rations? Who would decide who deserved sustenance and water when supplies dwindled? A great cacophony erupted in the antechamber. The chief Charter keeper interjected and declared that such calculations were unthinkable, and that the entire colony would have sustenance and water, and surely a solution would be reached before such time as resources ran out. Many of us applauded the Charter keeper and some declared loudly that Eden Prime would prevail. One of us stood up and asked why the Charter had not warned us of such a disaster? Why had we not been more prepared? Why were failsafes not put in place? How is it that the possibility of such a catastrophe had not been on our minds, never been entertained? A clangorous uproar briefly swelled in the antechamber and the Charter keeper bellowed for silence.

"We must not blame our Earth Parents for this misfortune," she said grandly. "Mars holds many secrets that our Earth Parents could not have known. Rest assured: We will prevail! We are braver, purer, than any humans to live before us. No other beings in history have accomplished what we have. This land, these tunnels, are truly ours, more so than any claim any human in any time could ever make. We were the first and only living organisms to ever be here. We have carved with our own hands a paradise out of lifeless rock. We may struggle in the time ahead, but we will do so for great purpose. Please know, my comrades, that our hardship will not be in vain! For our struggle is not merely for our survival, but for the glory of the human race!"

We erupted in rousing applause and cheers, not only for the Charter keeper's words, but for our own resilience and fortitude and magnificent purpose. The tunnelers declared that there was a small supply of lamps used for excavation that could be powered by manual cranking. They would distribute these to various vocational sectors. We returned to our vocational chambers and prepared vigorously for glorious triumph over the darkness.

There was no way to measure time in the darkness. The tunneling lights were requisitioned by the resource managing sectors as they sought novel solutions to sustain our colony in the dark. The rest of us, though, had to adjust to the dark. We began to hallucinate, many of us: balls of light, streaks of light, sounds that weren't there. In the absence of many humming machines, the footsteps and muffled voices echoed clangorously through our tunnels, the sounds coming from every direction all at once. Rest became elusive, the line between sleep and consciousness could not be easily defined. We moved carefully, our hands following the contours of the walls, firmly grabbing every ladder rung, listening carefully for the familiar voice of comrades who might re-center us upon disorientation.

My apprentice and I struggled to keep records in the dark, thought of how we might write clearly without sight. If we could no longer read the records of colonists past, what purpose did we have? We speculated that our records might be forever trapped inside the computers that no longer worked. But our duties could not be abandoned; keeping this history of our colony was of no less importance than preparing sustenance or managing the oxygen. Why, then, were the tunneling lamps never shared with us? Indeed, many of us asked these questions of purpose and value in the dining chamber as we wondered if our sustenance portions were shrinking.

In our sleeping chambers we exchanged stories among our cohorts of strange sensations and thoughts that arose in the dark. Some spoke of a tightness in their chests, or pain in their abdomen, or losing control of their breathing, or wordless sounds falling from their mouths and water falling from their eyes. Others spoke of thoughts that they could not stop, voices in their heads they did not recognize, voices that told them they would be retired prematurely, that they were all alone, that they were irrecoverably far away from something undefinable. Others still spoke of a heat that built in their spine, of clenching their fists and jaws without their willing it, or an uncanny feeling as if they were about to explode. There were also strange desires to break things, or use their voices loudly, or feel the bodies of their comrades, or stranger still, to breathe deeply of their scent and bite them. I'd heard similar talk from breeders before their memories were reset. As the elder record keeper I was one of the few allowed to see the breeders after they were sequestered. I collected brief interviews along with data recorded by caregivers and entered it into our database. I knew, too, that the implants were deactivated with beams of light shone into the eyes. I speculated that perhaps our implants were photosensitive, activated or charged by the red lights that used to illumine our colony. If so, why would this be kept secret from us? If it was unknown to the record keepers, then surely it was unknown to all of us.

During one sustenance service, an apprentice Charter keeper announced that there would be an assembly in the antechamber following sustenance consumption. We proceeded to the antechamber where two portable tunneling lamps illumined the space in a faint blue glow. When all had arrived and were seated on the floor, the chief Charter keeper stood up and welcomed us and praised our remarkable fortitude in spite of the darkness.

"We have heard tell of uncanny sensations in the dark. Hallucinations of mind and body, strange urges akin to those described by our Earth Parents. Under times of great stress, my comrades, it is possible that our implants struggle to maintain control of our limbic systems. But remember who we are! It is not merely the implants which make us indomitable. The

Charter reminds us that we are of superior genetics, our Earth Parents the finest specimens the Earthlings could collect. We were chosen — chosen, my comrades! — to extend the human race beyond the confines of our ravaged home, to conquer the vast unknown of our galaxy. We can — we must! — remain in control! Our feeble primal impulses are no match for our unconquerable wills!"

We cheered uproariously and were grateful for our Earth Parents, proud of our transcendent purpose. We heard updates from resource managers and they assured us that after new calculations, there would be sufficient resources to survive until communication with Earth could be established, and better yet, there was hope that, in fact, power could be restored sooner than that. We cheered wildly for these accomplishments, eager to believe that our tribulations would soon be over.

But the applause was interrupted. A voice forcefully bellowed: "My comrades! My comrades! Things are not as they seem!" Silence fell over us and a senior tunneler stood standing. "Why should our implants fail us in the dark? Why, suddenly, are the resource calculations different? My comrades, this catastrophe was no accident! No natural disaster! We will not survive this, and our resource managers are lying to us! They, too, know that we are doomed!" We gasped and guffawed and chattered with those around us. The elder Charter keeper demanded the tunneler be silent and tried to explain that the darkness is causing unprecedented effects on our minds and we must be strong to resist them. But the tunneler would not be silenced.

"I'll have you know, comrades, that for the last several Earth Years we tunnelers have been finding less and less selenium. This last transaction we acquired barely one crate's worth."

The elder Charter keeper tried again to interrupt him, but a senior sustenance grower insisted that The Charter gives the right for anyone to speak at assembly.

"Have any of us ever truly considered why we collect selenium, a mineral our Earth Parents tell us is useless to us? Or why Earthlings travel incredible tracts of space to collect it?"

"This is foolish nonsense!" one of us declared. "We know that the Earthlings are governed by their animal urges. The Earth Parents told us that they exchange selenium for personal possessions. There are no secrets to be uncovered here!"

"But why, then," the tunneler went on, "would Earthlings send us implants to control those urges? If they themselves see no need for these implants, if these implants in fact make us superior to them, why give them to us? Why not use them for their own benefit?"

A great murmuring arose among us as we repeated these questions to our neighbors and stammered over incomplete and unconvincing answers.

"Oh, my comrades," he bellowed over the din, "is it not possible that we are enslaved in the same way as Earthlings of old? That we are nothing but pawns in an Earthling capital enterprise? That it was the magnets the Earth ships used to collect our selenium that destroyed our electricity?" We broke into uproar, the elder Charter keeper called for order, but the tunneler continued, shouting over the cacophony. "Is it not possible that our Earth Parents came here to create a self-perpetuating source of free labor? We have exhausted the selenium, we have outlived our purpose, and it is easy enough for them to bury us alive!"

Three of us attempted to restrain the tunneler and coerce his silence, but more of us came to the tunneler's aid. And so began the first episode of open violence in the history of Eden Prime. The tunneling lamps were broken and we were once again sealed in darkness. The chaos was appalling. The collective panic of our entire colony stampeded through the antechamber. 12 of us died. Many were injured, some grievously, and the howls of our wounded comrades echoed interminably through the tunnels, sounds only previously heard after accidents in tunnels and ladder shafts, but now amplified to deafening levels. The wordless sounds of suffering followed us from end to end, down to our lowest reaches, and Eden Prime was no more.

I can no longer speak for all of us. We are no longer one colony, but two. Some of us chose to follow the tunneler, believing that the Charter is nothing but a grand deception, that in fact we are the victims of rapacious Earthlings. Most of us, though, remained loyal to the Charter, confident that we were still the captains of our fate, still the bold pioneers responsible for the destiny of all humankind. As the record keeper, I maintained neutrality and sought to record the evolution of both factions.

At first the separatists retreated to the lower reaches of the colony where they could guard the ladder shafts from intruders. The loyalists maintained control of the upper colony, chiefly the sustenance reserves. The loyalists rallied behind the Charter keepers who feared that the separatists, in their derangement, might attempt to destroy the colony. The only viable way to ensure the survival of the colony, they insisted, was their extermination. The loyalists endeavored to starve them into submission — their hunger would either drive them to swear their allegiance to the Charter and accept the error of their thoughts, or they would become weak enough to be easily dispatched.

But the darkness hid allegiances just as well.

Separatists could easily infiltrate the loyalist sector by silently blending with their comrades. However, the remaining mining lamps fixed on the sustenance stockpile made outright theft impossible. The separatists' first mission was obvious and successful. The sustenance reserves were pillaged, and many more colonists were injured and killed in the chaos. It was unclear if any mining lamps survived, but if so, they were kept hidden and secret.

The loyalists responded by breaking the glass of all the lights that once lit our tunnels and scattering it at strategic lines so that they could hear if any separatists attempted to breach their borders. Many separatists were captured in that initial raid, and they were stripped of their boots so that they could not safely pass the barriers of crushed glass. The smell of death and rotting flesh crept through every tunnel and sickened many, adding only to the foul stenches that made every breath a sacrifice. The captured separatists were forced to crank the air filtration fans until they collapsed, but they laughed all the while, saying "just like old times! How good to be a slave again!" And they would continue to laugh as they were beaten by their once intimately known comrades.

Their words did not go unheard, though, and many loyalists began to question the Charter. They would whisper among themselves, unsure of who could be trusted. More and more loyalists crossed over the lines of glass and sought answers from the senior tunneler, who was hidden and guarded in the lowest reaches of the colony.

I, too, made this pilgrimage down the many ladder shafts and new tunnels until an apprentice tunneler led me to the comrade whose ideas dissolved our colony. It must be stated that this senior tunneler and I belong to the same cohort. We had been comrades for our entire lives, and we knew each other as we knew ourselves. In this unfinished chamber, I called to him in the dark, and I moved towards his familiar voice.

"Comrade," I said. "What have you done?"

"I have shaken us awake, my comrade. I have loosed the invisible chains of our Earthling captors. I have found the weak link, and I will pull it until we are free."

"But how can you be so sure? Is it not possible that the darkness is deceiving your mind?"

"Is it not possible that it was the lights that were deceiving our minds? Is it not possible that only now are we able to think clearly?"

"But my comrade, there are many gaps in your theory."

"Are there?"

"Certainly. If your theory that we are being retired by an Earthling capitalist enterprise is true, why would they not simply kill us all at once? Destroy the entire colony with fire?"

"Because then they would also destroy the many tools and machines and computers and perhaps even implants which they will surely reuse in their next colony. To let us kill each other costs them nothing."

"Of what next colony do you speak?"

"Oh, my comrade," he said. "We are not the first Eden Prime. And we will not be the last. Surely this planet is pockmarked with the mass graves of many enslaved humans."

"But why, if we are merely slaves, would they give us the knowledge to recognize our condition? Why would we read many histories of Earth during our vocational formation? Why allow us to view images of Earth and Mars? Why study our ancestor's urges and emotions? Why emphasize their triumphs and follies and collapse? Why not limit us to the scientific knowledge required to mine selenium?"

"Think, my comrade: Do you believe that the entirety of human knowledge could be accessed on our scholastic computers? If not, who selected the texts and images we studied? Why would those be the texts and images selected by our Earthling overlords? How can we even know if anything contained in those computers is true? Is it not possible that every word of it was fabricated, carefully crafted to manipulate us into believing that we have some grand, noble purpose, unite us around a common enemy, give us rational justification for our complete and total isolation, for our implants, for the paste we must eat to stay alive? Are you not curious what they chose to omit? It seems to me, comrade, that a slave who loves his cage will never try to escape."

"But my comrade! The story of our Earth Parents is equally plausible. How can you be so sure that it is all a grand deception?"

"I cannot be sure, my comrade. This is precisely my point. We have always been certain of everything. Far too certain. And this, to me, is proof that we have been deceived."

I was overcome by a strange tension in my muscles and an urge to speak loudly. "And now what, comrade? Whether you are right or wrong, we are still doomed, but because of your reckless speculation we are doomed, too, to a suffering worse than anything the Earthlings could impose on us. At least we had each other!"

"Did we have each other, comrade? Now that our implants have failed, it seems that our limbic systems produce strange thoughts, strange questions. Thoughts and questions which make us unique. Without our impulses and urges and doubts and peculiar sensations, are we anything more than machines? We knew each other only as well as we knew the other tools in this mine."

"Perhaps you are correct, comrade. It seems I do not know you."

"Not yet, anyway. When we escape this prison we will finally meet each other in earnest."

"Escape? You said yourself that we have been buried alive. There is no way for us to survive on the surface."

"But my comrade, perhaps there is. Have you never considered that perhaps we are still on Earth?"

I was silent, overcome by a strange electricity in my spine.

"Think, my comrade: Is the narrative of our galactic pioneering only more manipulation? To deceive us into believing we are exceptional? Is it not suspicious that pride is one of the impulses not suppressed by our implants?"

"But my comrade, the red soil of Mars surrounds us!"

"And how are we to know for sure that the soil of Earth is not red? How are we to know that the image in the periscope is not an Earthling fabrication? I tell you comrade, we cannot. Is it not suspicious that we have no access to the surface? No exposure suits like the ones our Earth Parents supposedly wore? Why are the selenium elevator shafts unscalable, unusable without the magnetic pull of the Earthling space vessel? But if there was a way in, there must be a way out. All we must do is find the vault sealed behind the walls of the antechamber, open it, and climb to freedom."

"And if you are wrong, we will all die instantly!"

"Then we are doomed regardless."

"You fool! We could survive until the Earthlings send help!"

"I doubt that very much."

"How, then, do you propose to find this vault? It has been sealed since before the Alpha cohort was born."

"If anyone knows the location of the vault, it would be the record keeper."

My abdomen sank in an unfamiliar way. Two comrades seized me from behind and began to drag me by the arms.

"The loyalists will eventually learn of our plan and seek to end your life. You will be safe here."

They locked me in a bare chamber, alone. Two comrades guarded me, and I was fed sustenance periodically. I was often beaten by comrades with whom I once shared sustenance. They demanded answers that I did not possess. I can't say how much time passed, but my hair had grown many centimeters. My teeth had been broken, and my nose often leaked blood and shrieked in pain with each breath. I thought endlessly on my comrade's wild conjectures. Try as I might, though, I was unable to prove him wrong, even to myself. Perhaps he was right — why would the Earth Parents have gone to such lengths to make this colony inescapable? Why build over the only entrance to the surface? Why hide its location from all future cohorts? For what my captor would not believe is that I did not know the location of the surface vault. None of us did. Somewhere behind the walls of the antechamber likely, but where exactly was unknown.

There were times in that darkness when I felt weightless, suspended in oblivion. Sometimes I had the sensation that the ground beneath me may vanish at any moment, that I was falling down some interminable ladder shaft. I became dizzy, unsure if I was upside down, and would lie like a puddle in the blackness. I wished to give in to the darkness, merge with it and disappear entirely, but when I overheard that separatist comrades had begun excavating the antechamber, something stirred in me. I believed the colony could still be saved. I did what I thought was necessary.

"Comrade," I said to one of my guards. "Comrade, I cannot keep this secret any longer. I must tell you the truth."

He approached and ordered me to speak.

"The tunneler, our comrade who believes we are on Earth, he is not who he seems."

"How do you mean?"

"Is it not conspicuous how prepared he was during the final assembly in the antechamber? Is it not strange how easy it is for comrades to leave the upper colony and join him? Why do they not make assaults on the lower colony or seek to convince comrades to return to the Charter? How is it that separatists were able to retake the antechamber so easily?"

"What are you saying, comrade?"

"I am saying that in fact our tunneler comrade is in league with the loyalists! They calculated that there were only enough resources for the survival of half the colony, meaning that half of the colony must perish if the others are to survive until rescue. So they have enlisted the tunneler to lead half of us astray, lead half of us to a frozen death on the surface of Mars. Like he says of the imaginary capitalist Earthlings, it is easier to allow us to exterminate ourselves!"

This comrade conferred with the other guard, and she agreed that indeed, she had held her suspicions about the tunneler.

"You must let me escape," I pleaded. "Share the truth with your comrades, but do not let the tunneler know of your insight, or you will share a fate similar to mine."

They declined to release me at first, but some time later, I heard that the chamber door was not shut after my sustenance was served. I slipped into the tunnels and walked delicately, tactfully through the darkness. I manipulated my voice to convince the comrades who guarded the ladder shafts that I was an apprentice custodian, that I had been assigned to surreptitiously collect information on the loyalists above.

As I made my way through the tunnels, my fingertips dragging across the cold, rough walls of the lower colony, I began to wonder if in my mendacity I had accidentally stumbled upon the truth. What if, indeed, the senior tunneler was but a pawn in a loyalist conspiracy to dispatch the faithless? What if, in fact, there was nothing wrong with the generator and this entire calamity was a scheme to reduce our numbers? I began to tremble. My heart beat rapidly, loudly, and I struggled to breathe. Who was left for me to trust? Where was I headed? I sank to the ground with my back against the wall. Many tears fell from my eyes and I beckoned for someone, anyone, to guide me, for I had wholly lost my way.

After much feeble groping in the dark, I ascended to the middle levels. Here I encountered stenches so foul that my eyes burned, that my very brain was set alight. Weak voices of comrades I once knew begged for sustenance and water. I heard them drag themselves after me, beg me to carry them as their feet had been shredded by broken glass. One grabbed my ankle and implored me to go no further. I recognized this voice as if it were my own.

"Comrade," I said. It was my apprentice whom I had schooled since her initiation.

"Please, comrade," she said, "I hoped that you had died in the lower colony. I hoped that you would never learn what happened here."

After the separatist raid and the destruction of the mining lamps, what sustenance remained began to dwindle, stolen and hoarded by separatists and loyalists alike. The Charter keepers insisted that they and the resource managers requisition the majority of the remaining sustenance. Without ample sustenance for themselves, the elder Charter keeper had said, they could not ensure the survival of the colony.

"We became weak, delirious, enraged. Those of us who dissented were seized, our boots removed, and forced to crank the ventilators. The tunnel leaving the ventilation chambers was scattered with crushed glass such that escape without injury was impossible. Yet we were fed such little sustenance that some of us did take our chances to horrific ends. Those first most desperate of us encountered pain the likes of which we could scarcely comprehend. They collapsed in their agony only to fall on more glass. Some tried still to crawl, dragged by some instinct, some impulse that no implant could suppress. The screams. The howls. Sounds that echoed in our minds even in silence. Sounds that subsumed us in the same way as the dark. They begged for mercy, for forgiveness. They begged for death. They asked why. Pleaded to know why. And they continued to do so as their minds became soft and microbes consumed their wounds. All the while, the rest of us churned the ventilators and asked their same questions only in silence. But as time progressed we received less sustenance at longer, unpredictable intervals. We used violence to secure portions for ourselves. The urges," she said. Her voice quivered, a strange silence overtook her. "These urges, these thoughts, these sensations…" She began to weep and make wordless sounds.

I bade her continue. "What drove you to cross the glass?" I asked, squatting down at eye level despite our blindness, shaking her by her shoulders.

"One of us was killed in such a struggle," she said slowly through heavy breaths. "And we consumed his flesh for sustenance."

I stepped back.

"I understand now," she said. "I believe now. The Charter speaks truth. The Earth Parents loved us. The implants *were* our liberation."

I retreated from my apprentice. Her pleas echoed after me down the tunnel. She implored me to record her testimony so that she may fulfill her final duty to Eden Prime.

I found my way at last to the record chamber. Here I recorded the final epoch of Eden Prime with great care. I have heard word that the separatists located the vault and are attempting to gain entry to the surface shaft. Some separatists, motivated by the doubt I sowed in their minds, intervened violently to no avail.

I will not go to their aid, I will do nothing more. To assert my convictions, if I had any left, would be merely vanity. I hope only for respite from this wretched imprisonment, from these tunnels, from the darkness, from our most sordid biology. My comrades' pursuit of the surface will liberate us one way or another.

I know not whether we are the victims of savage Earthlings or poor fortune. Whether our purpose was grand or trivial. Whether deception is mercy or torture. Whether it is our impulse towards certainty or our impulse towards doubt which is more pernicious. I do know, though, which of those is more painful, for beyond the hunger and terror and selfishness, crueler than all the pain and dread, is the doubt that undergirds it all. And whether this doubt was our salvation or our damnation, I will learn imminently.

I can hear the clangor of pickaxes and tools echo from the antechamber. These will be my final words, this epistle the final record of Eden Prime. Soon enough light will re-enter these tunnels, and I shudder to think of what it will reveal.

Shiva the Destroyer

July 15

Ran into Jacob Williams at Safeway yesterday. He looks more or less the same. Still kind of fat. Still works at the sawmill. I told him I was back in town for a few weeks to visit my parents. Didn't feel like telling him I was between jobs. He asked with a smirk if I'd turned into an East Coast dandy or something. He insisted I come over for drinks, meet up with some old friends who still lived in town. I said sure. So tonight I met him and Tyler Cox and Aaron Washburn on Jacob's back patio. I hadn't seen either of them since at least 2015. Tyler's a Second Amendment nut job now, and Aaron married Abby, which I guess made me happy to hear. Reminiscing about high school was more fun than I'd like to admit, especially after a few beers. We were getting good and drunk when someone mentioned Kurt.

"Have you heard from him lately? At all?" I think Aaron brought it up.

I had to think about it. Not since at least 2018. They made it sound like he'd fallen off the face of the Earth. I was a little embarrassed, to be honest. I should know what's up with Kurt. I owe him at least that much. Had it been that long since I'd tried to reach out to him? They went around the table speculating wildly: He'd changed his identity, he'd lost his mind and was living under a bridge in Portland, he'd finally gone and offed himself, which wasn't fucking funny and I told them so. That was the end of the night for me. I realized that they were probably just bitter that Kurt went to college and shook the dust of this sad little town off his boots. They probably said the same shit about me.

It got me thinking about Kurt, though. I sent him a text. I just gotta know he's all good.

July 17

Never heard from Kurt. Tried calling. The number was disconnected.

I'm actually worried. He's scared me like this before. I've been thinking a lot about the day he tried to kill himself. It was sophomore year. A few months after his mom had passed. He'd taken a handful of her expired cancer pain meds with a swig of vodka. I went over there after school looking for him. He had puke all over himself. Like all over the pillow and he'd rolled on top of it. And I shook him and like really fucking screamed at him. Screamed his name over and over. Like I was calling from the dark side of the tunnel with the light at the end of it. And I slapped him really hard and I started crying and I punched him in the face so hard I hurt my hand. And then he grunted and groaned. I called 911 and watched the paramedics plunge a hypodermic needle into his heart. And I honestly never forgave him for it.

July 18

My parents said the last they'd heard from Kurt was two years ago. A Christmas card from him and his roommates in Eugene. Mom was worried, too. Asked why I hadn't been in touch with him. Said I didn't know and got angry. I guess she feels like Kurt's kind of her son too. Foster son, maybe. I don't know what that relationship would feel like. But she cared enough for him to take him into our home for almost two years. She fed him and checked in on him, and drove him to the DMV when it was time for him to get his license. Kurt's dad went from being a heavy drinker to a full blown boozehound after Kurt's mom died. It was awful to watch. The grief. And his older brother was 26 and a fuck up. And Kurt was left all alone in that house with all that grief. He had me across the street. And Jacob down the street. And that was it really. And that wasn't much, because truth be told, I didn't really care. That kind of hardship, that kind of despair, was incomprehensible to me. I think I was angry with him for making me find him like that. That he would bail on me like that. That he was siphoning off my family's attention and eating the food in my kitchen. And things were never really the same. I pulled away, feeling justified in distancing myself from his bitter aloofness. One day we were playing Xbox and got in a fight. He was being an arrogant prick — he could be condescending like that — and said something about how I didn't know how good I had it, how I was sheltered and naive and how the world was going to eat me alive and shit me out. And I said, great, then I can be a piece of shit just like you.

We didn't talk for weeks after that. I'm pretty sure that was after graduation. So the summer before college. Which, now that I think about it, was a sad way for that to end.

But college was really good for him. He got out of Creswell. Got away from his family. Even if it was only 15 miles, Eugene was a world away.

Mom dug up the Christmas card. I'd met one of his roommates before. One of his college friends. The card had a return address. Headed to Eugene tomorrow.

July 19

Drive to Eugene was easy. I thought about the time I visited Kurt at U of O. Junior year. Our spring breaks lined up. We'd seen each other over the holidays in Creswell and promised to connect. So I drove into town to his off campus house to see what his life was like. I knew he was studying sociology, and I got the sense from his social media that he'd gone full leftist. And the thing with Kurt is that he's brilliant. Probably an actual genius. One of the smartest people I've ever encountered for sure. Even in elementary school you could tell he was on a different level. He was curious in a grand, cosmic way. There was a sort of feline shrewdness about him, and a seriousness that was maybe actually a kind of anger. He was also sensitive, timid. Scrawny and shy. He liked *Harry Potter* and *Lord of the Rings*. Couldn't care less about sports. He cried sometimes when kids gave him shit on the playground. Myself included. Actually, one time we were riding quad bikes with Jacob, and Jacob ran over a squirrel. Like, on purpose. He chased it down and ran over its back legs. But obviously it didn't die right away, and the three of us stood around staring at it while it spasmed and panicked and looked up at us with easily recognizable horror. And we were all kind of fucked up about it, even Jacob, but Kurt started crying. Full on water works. Jacob called him a fag and then Kurt started slapping and punching him, but Jacob was twice his size and able to just stiffarm him away. Jacob drove on and I watched from the seat of my quad bike as Kurt scooped the squirrel up and carried it off the gravel road and into the trees. I remember telling him consolingly that it would be a good dinner for a hawk, but he had nothing to say about that.

In high school we were in all the same honors classes together. I came to resent that he was smarter than me, how effortlessly he succeeded, how I needed to ask him for help more than I'd have liked. We still hung out to a degree. He'd be over at my house often enough to eat. We'd play video games or do homework. We didn't talk a lot, though. He retreated further into himself as high school went on, and I had no interest in drawing him back into the world.

When I saw him that time in college, though, he seemed different. Expansive. He was excited, agitated in a rousing sort of way. Between bong rips he'd rage against capitalism, colonialism, American exceptionalism. He'd predict the fall of western society, wax apocalyptic on the climate and the human condition. Advocate for Buddhism, feminism, marxism, anarchy.

We ate shrooms with two of his buddies and walked through town and down to the river. I think Kurt thought he was going to change the world. Rattle it like a broken vending machine. Kick it like a jukebox needing a restart. A part of me thought he would, too.

We kept in touch for a while after that. I think I visited him one other time the following summer. We'd try to schedule a phone call here and there but never follow through. He and his dad came over for Thanksgiving one year. He was working at a non-profit in Eugene. He seemed good. And that was the last time I saw him. His dad sold the house that summer and moved, I don't know where. Out of state I think. And that was four years ago.

I didn't think Kurt would be at the address on the Christmas card. It was unlikely his roommates were even still living there. And is eating shrooms together enough of a bond for his old roommate to remember me or want to talk to me? It was the only lead I had.

But sure enough, Riley remembered me. He welcomed me in graciously and boiled some water for tea. He hadn't heard from Kurt in a while himself, but he didn't seem especially worried. Apparently Kurt had gone off-grid intentionally. Riley himself had driven him to a farm somewhere in the Coast Range. And apparently all he had on him was a big backpack like he was about to do the Pacific Crest Trail. And that was a year and a half ago. No one's heard from him since. He said that Kurt left a box of stuff in the house for storage, but had donated or thrown out basically everything else. Riley figured he'd come back when he was ready. When I mentioned that the last time I'd heard from him was 2018, Riley said: "Oh shit."

"So you don't know about the protest?"

I said no and egged him on.

He'd gone up to Portland with some friends to march at a Black Lives Matter protest. That night he got fully brained by a cop. Like annihilated by a riot cop. He got shot in the face with a rubber bullet and when he was stumbling to get up, a cop cracked his head open with a baton and knocked him out cold. And then they handcuffed him. Riley said he saw the whole thing, but by that point Kurt was on the other side of the police line and there was nothing he could do.

He was in the hospital for seventeen days. He lost his left eye and his left orbital bone was broken pretty much in half. Or I guess he still has his eye, but he can't see out of it. It reshaped his whole face. Like, they had to put pins in his orbital bone. And the cop's baton fractured his skull. He had multiple surgeries. The nerves in his face were so damaged it gave him some kind of permanent Bell's Palsy. And because it was during Covid he wasn't allowed any visitors at all. He couldn't move his head or open his mouth. He just had to sit there, alone, in agony, with nothing but his grief and impotent rage.

Riley said he was different when he finally got discharged. Didn't talk. Didn't leave the house. Barely left his room from the sound of it. His face was black and blue for weeks and he had to wear a plastic face guard for just as long. The Bell's Palsy made it so that the left half of his face was paralyzed and droopy. Riley described him as "inaccessible." But not like despairing. And not vacant either. But serious. Brooding. I knew exactly what he was talking about. Like how he was for most of high school.

Riley still knew the name of the farm. It's some kind of off-grid organic deal. Somewhere between Philomath and Alsea. I looked it up. It's an actual farm. Looks like their main thing is blueberries. I gave them a call, but all I got was a message with rates for wholesale blueberries and hours for when prospective buyers can inspect the fields. I guess I'll be posing as a blueberry aficionado on Thursday.

Before I left Eugene, Riley asked me about Kurt's stuff. He thought he'd have been back for it by now, but he's moving out next month and didn't especially want to haul it along with him. I told him I'd hold onto it. A U-Haul box, mostly books I think, based on the weight. My old bedroom is mostly for storage these days anyway.

July 21

The box wasn't taped shut, so I don't feel especially bad about looking through it. It was full of books. Most of them seemed to be from college. Howard Zinn, bell hooks, Adorno and Horkheimer. Nietzsche, Sartre, Deleuze. Lots of Foucault. Thick with annotations, all of them. A printed out copy of his under-grad thesis — a 130 page essay titled "Neoliberal Economics and the Commodification of Identity: How Late Capitalism Subverts Revolution."

There was also a stack of notebooks. Spiral, college-ruled, three-subject. These I was a little less inclined to pore over, but my curiosity got the better of me. I flipped through them tenderly as if they were museum pieces. Like I was wearing white gloves to study some arcane medieval text. Half of them were notes from college courses, chaotically intermingled with what seemed to be journal entries or reflections relating to the material. I found myself wondering if I'd ever filled a single notebook cover to cover like this. If I'd ever even had this many thoughts. I didn't earnestly read any of them; I was mostly transfixed by the totality of his ideas, the urgency with which he needed to get them out of his head, the inexhaustible clangor of his inner monologue.

The remaining notebooks were more traditional journals. Rather than recording daily updates, there'd be one entry every few weeks, anywhere from three to a dozen pages of tight, single-spaced script. Blue or black ink. Sometimes pencil. I tried not to read anything too closely, but I got the sense that none of it was especially intimate. This was a catalog of ideas rather than feelings, of exploration rather than confession. None of it was rambling or fatuous, but chaotic in a spirited sort of way nonetheless. Lengthy tirades about current events, culture war fulminations, climate despair, analyses of garish media, critiques of books and movies he either loved or hated. Frequent philosopher name drops. He was a man possessed by radical notions of dissent and rebellion, dystopian prophecies, outright disgust with the machinations of modern society. But most of all, he seemed utterly bewildered, driven mad, even, by how no one else seemed to notice. How everyone else was blind to the injustice and lunacy and cruelty of the world. How nobody cared. He seemed tormented by a big-picture perspective too vast and complex to articulate to anyone, even himself.

The last notebook was from 2020. I skipped ahead to March and then April and May. His final entry before the protest was a doozy — a furious, fluvial meditation on power and oppression, on police states and fascists and the decay of community at the hands of capitalism. "We have forgotten that we belong to each other, that we have been entrusted to each other," he wrote, "distracted too long by the bright lights and cheap novelties of a rapacious system that never cared — that cannot care — about dignity."

The next entry was from August. It said only this:

"I'm a fool," he wrote. "I'm a goddamned fool. I've been wrong all along. The world ended a long time ago."

After that came his final entry, dated November 5. "I'm tired of people being ugly to each other," he wrote. "I can't take it anymore."

He went on to outline his exit from society. How he would live off the grid, off the land, and disappear forever. His last words: "I hope they all forget my name."

July 23

I really hoped Kurt would be at the blueberry farm. I rehearsed all the things I'd ask him. I prepared myself to not react upon seeing his injuries. I really just wanted to give the guy a big hug. Not ask him to come back or anything, or try to change his mind. Just let him know that he was important to me. When I passed through Corvallis I started to get nervous. What if he didn't want to see me? What if he pretended he didn't know me? Fair enough, I told myself. I promised I'd respect that.

The farm was deep in the Coast Range. I lost cell service a full half hour before I got there. It was way off the main highway, and the road turned to gravel and wound around the mountains for the last two miles. The forest was so dense that I had a hard time imagining a farm up there, but after a final steep push up this gravel road, a glorious meadow opened up and a rough hewn sign welcomed me to Blue Moon Farm. I passed a small apple orchard and a chicken coop before ending up in front of the farmhouse. Vines grew thickly over the trellised patio and up the walls. Shrubs bloomed along the side of the house, pink flowers hung from beams over the patio. Hummingbirds flitted around dangling nectar feeders. It was incredibly quiet. Past the farmhouse was a barn and horse stables. An enormous white horse stared at me from across the corral a hundred feet away. On the other side of the circular drive was a machine bay with a tractor and a windrower and a wall full of tools. Beyond that was a couple acres of berry fields, and beyond that, a pasture. I half expected to catch a glimpse of Kurt emerging from the stables or rising above the blueberry bushes.

The door to the farmhouse opened behind me and a stolid old man in Carhart overalls and a wide-brimmed hat asked if he could help me. I said I was looking for Kurt and his demeanor softened.

"I always figured someone would come looking for him," he said, but mostly to himself. It seemed, though, that Kurt was long gone.

His name was Alan, and he asked me to follow him out to the field while he checked his irrigation.

"Probably the best farmhand I ever had," he said. "Really impressive guy. His first week here he fixed my windrower for me. Read the manual and fixed it. Couldn't believe it."

He asked how I knew Kurt and I told him. "Well, I'm glad someone's out there looking for him," he said. "I always got the impression that he didn't have any people. He was here for a whole year and I didn't learn hardly anything about him. But like I said, he was a fine worker. He even managed to reclaim all that wooded property on the other side of the pasture." He pointed with his chin towards the tree line. Apparently there had been a cabin back there once upon a time, but the whole space had been choked out by blackberry vines and other noxious weeds. Kurt took it upon himself to terraform it all. Hack back all the brush, carve out a trail system. "He built an entire homestead back there," he said. "Got the water running again, renovated the cabin. All by himself. The only time he asked for help was when he needed propane or lumber driven back there. Incredible, really. I've got my new farmhand living back there now."

Alan got down on his knees to turn the irrigation off. I looked out at the blueberries and the pasture and the woods. Good for you, Kurt, I thought. I think I even envied him.

I asked him if he knew where Kurt is now.

"I know where I dropped him," he said. "He wanted to hitchhike down to Grants Pass, but I wouldn't hear of it. And you know what," he said suddenly. "I'll bet the directions are still in the glovebox."

And sure enough, in the glovebox of his F150 was a crumpled piece of notebook paper, the kind that you might write a shopping list on. And in Kurt's handwriting were directions to a place without a name. Not a short trip. And I don't know southern Oregon at all.

On the drive home I wondered if maybe I should just leave him alone. He'd gone to some serious lengths to disappear. Hell, me showing up looking for him might enrage him. Maybe it's better to just let sleeping dogs lie.

July 27

Drive took about five hours. Hotter than hell, forecast at 110, hot even for southern Oregon.

I was on the last step of the directions, taking some unnamed dirt road through the wilderness, again up a mountain when two guys riding ATVs and strapped with AR-15s came around the bend. They had tinted sunglasses and baseball caps and neck gaiters pulled over their faces. No camo or uniforms or anything, just t-shirts and shorts and work boots. One of them dismounted and I realized that the road was too narrow to turn around, too windy to reverse. He tapped on the window with the muzzle of his gun and waited for me to lower it. "I think you made a wrong turn, friend."

I was about to shit my pants to be honest, and all I could do was blurt out "I'm here to see Kurt."

He was quiet for a minute and looked to the guy behind him, still on his ATV. "Like I said, you made a wrong turn."

"No, wait." I showed him the directions and said "it's even in Kurt's handwriting. Come on."

He looked it over and walked back to his buddy. They examined the paper together, conferenced, and then they both walked back over to me. The second one took off his sunglasses to reveal a lazy, half-opened left eye.

"Unbelievable," he said. He pulled down the gaiter.

It was Kurt all right. The rubber bullet had left a kind of crater or divot just south of his left temple, and he had a thick beard to obscure the paralysis of the left half of his mouth. His hair was long and he was fit in a way I'd never seen before, his posture almost imposing. It was hard to imagine him as anything other than the bony bookworm I grew up with.

"Kurt," I said. "Thank God."

"What are you doing out here?" He was more incredulous than irate.

"Been worried about you."

"No need for that," he said and turned to the other guy. "He's cool. Let him up."

They revved their ATVs and I followed them up the mountain another half mile or so. The dry ponderosas suddenly gave way to fields of weed. Acres of weed. Millions of dollars of weed. There were greenhouses and barns and machinery and pickup trucks and quad bikes. We slowed to a stop before a cul-de-sac of numerous barn-like buildings all with solar panels on the roofs. Kurt was talking closely with the other guy as he waved subtly to me to get out of my car.

"You need to give him your keys and driver's license. And your phone." I protested, but there was something commanding in his voice, and his face was expressionless, stone-like. He said they have to make sure I don't leave with anything. I dropped it all in the other guy's hand and watched him walk into a barn that served as what I can only describe as an armory. There were literally rows of assault rifles, shotguns, handguns up on a pegboard. I'm pretty sure I saw a grenade launcher.

"You can't go in there," Kurt said when he caught me looking.

I followed him on a dirt path into the woods. The heat was staggering. The sky was hazy with the smoke of nearby wildfires. Very little stirred. The crops bent languidly in unison by a breeze almost too soft to feel.

"I take it you met Alan," he said. "How long have you been looking for me?"

I told him.

We kept walking through the forest where people lived dispersed in campgrounds deep into the trees. "Campgrounds" doesn't do it justice. Some had little tiny houses or vans but others were like outdoor lounges. Tents and tarps and hammocks and overhangs. We passed a communal outhouse and shower area. In the distance through the trees was a dusty meadow and some kind of Bronze Age-looking longhouse.

"Well, welcome," he finally said when we came to a stop. I had to look around before realizing I was standing in his camp. "It's good to see you," he said, a small smile curled up on his right side.

I told him I missed him, and that he looked fucking great, and I was just so happy to see him. I gave him a big back-slapping hug and held on tight for a minute.

I asked him how he was. He said "free."

We sat on big meditation cushions under a shade sail made of a psychedelic tapestry strung up in the trees. Kurt sat cross-legged, almost in a lotus position. He bent to his right and opened a small wooden chest he said he made himself and pulled out a bowl and a grinder. He explained that the farm was a legal grow operation, but there were some things he couldn't tell me: How many people live there, how much money they pull, who owns the property, where they draw their water from. He could tell me, though, that it was a community organized around preparing for societal collapse, which the weed farm financially supported.

"Like a doomsday end-of-the-world thing?" I asked.

"No," he said. "Worlds end everyday." He lit the bowl, took a sharp hit, and let the smoke diffuse slowly out of his mouth. "My world ended sophomore year of high school. Then it ended again in 2020. I got tired of pretending otherwise."

He passed the bowl to me. I asked him how he ended up here. In stoic, hushed tones, he said something like this:

"When I was in the hospital I was more embarrassed than anything. They had to wire my jaw shut after resetting my orbital, and my head was fastened into one of those birdcage things. And it was like I was in time out or something. Like I just had to sit there and think about what I'd done. For two and a half weeks. And it all just felt so fucking stupid. It was like I was in there for trying to headbutt my way through a brick wall. Like the doctors and nurses were all laughing at me behind their masks and hazmat gear. What an idiot!" He got agitated here, animated like I remember him in college. "What kind of stupid fucking delusion was I under to think that that protest would have ended any differently? Instead of being angry at that faceless riot cop, or the system, or Big Brother or whatever, I was just angry at myself. I did this to myself," he said, pointing at his face.

He took another deep hit from the bowl and allowed himself to relax.

He was so disgusted with all of it, he said. Society, philosophy, humanity. He wanted to exit the system. Disappear entirely. Return to a state of nature. So he found the blueberry farm.

He told me about the horses. He fed them twice a day and spent a lot of his free time just watching them. The bigger horse bullied the shit out of the smaller one, he said. "Relentlessly," he said. "Terrorized him. Would eat all his food and corner him and not let him out of the corral. Bite him, kick him, chase him around." The big one was named Zeke and the smaller one Izzy. It turns out all horses are like that, he said. All animals, actually. They naturally establish dominance and organize around it. Hierarchy is a fact of the animal kingdom, he said, all the way down to bees and ants.

He went on to talk about where the phrase "pecking order" comes from, how the smaller chickens would get pecked at viciously and just stand there and take it, and then peck on the chicken smaller than them. How parasitic wasps, the farm's organic pest control, lay eggs inside caterpillars that are eventually eaten from the inside out by the larvae. How the barn cats would savor playing with the mice and voles before finally eviscerating them. How flies could disappear that same shredded carcass in a few hours. How hatefully sharp gooseberry thorns are, pointed at exactly the right angle to slice open the muzzle of a hungry deer. How quickly and rapaciously the blackberry vines would suffocate and smother an entire garden.

He went off-grid to escape the violence and ugliness of society only to realize that all he had done was "zoom in on this infinitely repeating fractal pattern," he called it. "Violence. Everywhere, in everything. It's the underlying source code of the entire universe. Combustion and collision. Conflict and consumption. If you zoom in to the subatomic level, you'll see that everything is a function of violence. All matter, all energy, everything in the universe. Atoms and electrons exploding and colliding. It's how every cell in your body makes energy, ripping molecules apart and slamming them back together again. Sex, birth, the germ warfare forever teeming inside you, all objectively and profoundly violent. Same thing if you zoom all the way out. Empires, economies, all of human history. Every landscape, every mountain range, every coast line, formed by earthquakes and volcanoes and oceans, the fury and power of which you can't imagine. Stars, planets, asteroids, supernovas, the Big Bang. All this daylight, every beautiful sunset, every star in the sky, is the afterglow of inconceivably explosive violence."

I had to chew on all that for a minute, stoned as I was. But I challenged him. What about the beauty, the harmony, the peace and tranquility of the farm?

"Oh, it's beautiful all right," he said. "The horses, the cats, the landscape of trees and plants that outcompeted everything else, all fed in a primary, secondary, or tertiary way by the nuclear holocaust inside the sun. There's harmony and beauty in the blades of a windrower, too," he said. "But if you stick your hand in it, it won't hesitate to chew it off in order to keep the machine going." He talked about fixing the windrower, driving it, mowing the pasture. How he would watch the mice and snakes and birds that lived in the grass dart for safety or get mangled in the fourteen-foot blades. "And I became Shiva, destroyer of worlds."

He smoked more.

"And sure, the pasture looked beautiful after a mowing," he said. "But the horror..." He paused and watched the smoke dissipate. "There was no ignoring the horror behind it all."

I laid down in the dirt, my head on the meditation cushion, to let it all sink in. Kurt, too, was still.

"How did it feel?" I finally asked. "To be Shiva."

I looked up at him from the ground. He still sat with his legs folded, his spine straight. The purple psychedelic tapestry reflected in his sunglasses. He was silent for a moment.

"When I tried to kill myself in high school, it wasn't because I was depressed or didn't want to live anymore. I was just so angry. I just wanted to not be angry anymore. I was so angry that I would rather die than keep feeling that angry." He paused and looked away as if to gather himself. "But I had this horrifying thought, right before I passed out, that if I died angry, I would stay that way for all eternity. Be reborn even angrier. Be condemned to relive it all over and over again. Forever. Why would a world this mean be any different in death? So I guess I owe you one for saving me from that. I thought I could absolve my anger by conquering all the unfairness in life. Make it so there was nothing to be angry about anymore. But all I ended up doing was wedging my head inside the gears of a machine that stops for no one."

He tapped the ash out of the bowl and returned it to its box.

"But you know what," he finally said. "I'm not angry anymore."

He went back to the horses. How the big one dominated the small one, how the small one would cower and shake. How it was blind in one eye from an infection. "That bloody, fogged-over eye was just too on the nose," he said. "I just couldn't be that horse anymore."

He talked about building his homestead. How he cut back and dug out every last blackberry and thistle and poison oak in the woods, how he chopped down trees, flooded underground hornet nests with boiling water, refused to let nature reconquer his space.

A staccato drum line of gunfire rattled in the distance. Another one. I sat up with a start.

"Target practice," Kurt said.

I looked around and suddenly saw everything anew.

"Is this some kind of militia?" I asked.

"You could call it that," he said.

The sun was low in the sky and the heat of the day was fading. Kurt urged me to stay for dinner, stay the night, but I felt uneasy. I felt unsafe, to be honest. And I had a swooning, thumping headache from the heat and the weed and the vague malaise of Kurt's pessimism. It didn't seem like I had much of a choice about staying the night, seeing as my keys, phone, and license were locked up with an apocalypse-ready arsenal, and I was in no state to navigate back to civilization anyway.

I laid in the dirt a while longer. Kurt asked about me, my parents. He seemed genuinely interested. I gave him updates on current events. He listened intently without commenting. He showed me to the vegetable garden and the community long-house adorned with runic script and carved dragon heads like the kind you might see at the helm of a Viking warship.

We walked to a large pavilion in the meadow that served as an open-air mess hall. There was a short buffet of rice, beans, and steamed vegetables. We filled our waters from a spigot in the parched grass and ate at long picnic tables as other militia members came and went for dinner. Kurt introduced me to some of them. Men and women whose ages ran the spectrum. Some had buzz cuts, some had dreadlocks. I saw a handful of children running around. They were mostly welcoming, though, if a little leery. No one seemed brainwashed and I didn't hear any North Korea-style references to a beautiful, enlightened leader. It all seemed reasonably wholesome until it occurred to me that everyone was white. Coincidence, maybe. But at this point I really didn't want to learn too much. Whether they were simply preparing for societal collapse or actively agitating for it was unclear. In any case, Kurt seemed hungry for it.

At dark we returned to his campsite and smoked more. He finally took off his sunglasses and I could see from the strobes of the snapping lighter, the faint glow of the embers in the bowl, how half his face was frozen in a pained, defeated frown, his left eye gazing limply, morosely into the abyss below his feet. I slept restlessly in Kurt's hammock, feeling at times like I was lying suspended over oblivion, dangling like bait for some toothy monster of the unfathomable deep.

Kurt was up before sunrise, and I was eager to get up when I heard him stirring. He had greenhouse duty and would walk me back to the security station where I could pick up my things. I remembered to tell him about his box of books. He told me to throw them out. I said I wouldn't, and they'll be waiting for him.

"It was good to see you," he said and we hugged again. He said he was impressed by my effort to find him, but warned me against ever telling anyone. I gave him my word. As he started to walk away, I finally told him I was sorry.

"For what?" He asked.

For everything that'd happened to him. For his mom, for his face, for his tender heart that ruptured under the strain of it all. For not being a better friend when he needed me. That last one is the only one I said out loud. He looked away.

"All good," was all he said, and he disappeared into one of the barns.

I drove home without incident, without so much as a pit stop, wondering all the while if it was all somehow my fault.

August 4

Spent my last week at home with mom and dad. Didn't leave the house much. Went for a hike to Trestle Creek Falls. Helped mom in the garden. Grilled in the backyard a few times. Very grateful for my folks.

I told them that Kurt was working on a farm down south and doing well. They didn't ask much after that. But his cynicism has been rattling around my head all week. The problem is that I can't really say that any of his ideas are incorrect or untrue. But for all his sophistry and stoic absolutism, his new worldview boils down to "if you can't beat 'em, join 'em." Insipid, Darwinian nihilism forged under the weight of the many dominating forces that fall on us like gravity. But that, too, feels unfair. Perhaps a deeper truth buried under all his cosmic realpolitik is a truth that Kurt once surely knew but simply can't apply to himself, that hurt people hurt people. The tragedy being that Kurt won't acknowledge how hurt he is. Or that it's not his fault. Because on the other side of all his fatalistic insights about violence and power is the softness and vulnerability that makes us all victim to it. Life is delicate, tender, fragile — Shiva only brings it into sharp relief.

So I wrote Kurt a letter saying all that. And I conceded that he's not wrong about anything, but he has surely missed the point. And I said that in a world so harsh and vicious, the only decent thing to do is care. Care about people's pain. Care about their grief and anguish and suffering. And in a world of claws and fangs and thorns, the only true rebellion is a life of gentle compassion.

I folded it and put it on top of his journals and taped the box shut. A part of me is sure that he will be back for it one day. There is hope in the fact that he was able to discard all of his earthly possessions, but he couldn't let go of his ideas. If the Kurt I know is still in there, and I'm sure he is, I don't doubt that one day he'll find a wounded squirrel in the woods, cradle it in his hands, and weep for it. And the anger he has become numb to will thaw like frostbite, his heart will crack like a frozen pond in spring, and he will finally, truly, be free.